Grenades were going off all around them, and still they worked. Dan, looking on terrified and transfixed, was amazed that the people pulling the net could find the courage to keep on dragging it toward shore.

Suddenly, an explosion tore up the ground a few feet behind them.

That was all Dan could take. He erupted from his hiding place with a guttural scream and began running toward the others. Karen dropped her part of the net and turned to run for cover. Then she stopped in her tracks and hit the ground. Dan thought she had been hurt, but then he saw what she had seen. . . .

CYBORG COMMANDO™

BOOK 3

THE ULTIMATE PRIZE

by Pamela O'Neill
and Kim Mohan

Cover illustration by Janny Wurts

THE ULTIMATE PRIZE

A CYBORG COMMANDO™ Book

CHASE INTO SPACE is based on an original concept by Gary Gygax. The characters in this book are fictitious. Any resemblance to actual persons, living or dead, is purely coincidental.

First printing, April 1988
Printed in the United States of America

Distributed to the book trade by the Berkley Publishing Group, 200 Madison Avenue, New York NY 10016

9 8 7 6 5 4 3 2 1

ISBN: 0-441-84325-5

New Infinities Productions, Inc.
P.O. Box 657
Delavan WI 53115

For the people of planet Earth . . .

. . . because we're all in this together.

Other books in the
CYBORG COMMANDO™ series

Planet in Peril

Chase Into Space

Prologue

The Master faced two struggles.

One of them was happening on the surface of the planet Earth, where the creatures operating under Its control were having a more and more difficult time in their attempt to conquer and exterminate the human race.

The other struggle, the more intriguing and in many ways the more frustrating of the two, was taking place within Itself. For the first time in Its existence, the Master was subconsciously experiencing concepts and emotions that It, in all Its wisdom, could not easily find words to define.

It had never encountered this much resistance before, on any of the worlds It had chosen to conquer.

It had known anger before, but that anger had always been founded in arrogance: How could the natives of this world, or that one, have the audacity to suppose that they could stand against and overcome all the destructive force that It could bring to bear against them? Time and again the Master had become angry, and when that occurred It had simply stepped up the ferocity of Its onslaught and crushed the resistance.

It had felt something similar to self-doubt on several occasions before, but had always been able to convince Itself that It was not at fault. Even though It had virtually unlimited resources, It was always prudent in the employment of those resources; why expend twice as much force to accomplish a task when half as much would produce the desired result? When It had seemingly underestimated the strength of Its opponent, It would merely bring more force to bear — always expending enough, but never more than necessary, to cripple and annihilate whatever stood in the way. In the end, It had always been victorious, and had always been able to pride Itself on the brutally efficient use of the creatures, devices, and machines under Its control.

In fact, It had told Itself frequently, the only challenge It ever faced was in deciding just how much force would be needed to conquer a certain objective. Therefore, It could not be blamed — and should actually be commended — when Its initial invasion force did not succeed in conquering the world on which it descended. If a victory was ever won too easily, It would always wonder whether the conquest could have been achieved by the application of less force than It had used. The Master was ruthless and brutal, but It was not wasteful.

The dominant species of planet Earth had caused It some irritation, to put it mildly. The planet was into its third orbit around its star since the invasion had taken place, and still the Master's forces had not achieved their goal. The human race had actually managed to defeat some of Its minions and foil some of Its plans, mostly because of the use of strange constructs that seemed to be machines made in the image of men. The Master had become enraged when Its transport vessels were forced off the surface of the planet and then destroyed; such a thing had never happened before!

But It quickly regained Its composure — as all super-intelligent beings are supposed to do. What mankind had done would not alter the final outcome, because It had more resources that It could call into play, more tactics that It could employ. Compared to the power of these man-machines to resist, Its capabilities were limitless.

That is what It told Itself; that is the essence of the conscious thought that It devoted to the subject. But somewhere deep inside Its psyche, in a place that It was only vaguely aware of, other thoughts were taking shape.

It was becoming angry not out of arrogance, but out of frustration and . . . fear. It was becoming apprehensive; a small voice within Itself was forming questions It had never had to contend with before.

Had It made a wrong decision by selecting this planet for conquest?

Was it possible that the inhabitants of this planet also had resources and capabilities they had not yet called upon?

Was it conceivable that It might actually fail?

These questions, and others like them, had not yet made their way into Its consciousness. But they did exist, and sooner or later they would demand to be acknowledged — and answered.

1

March 17, 2037

"Now what's it doing?" S-24 whispered anxiously as he watched the creature scoop something up out of the water.

"Fishing, maybe? . . . Hell, I don't know!" W-105 speculated, then changed his answer when he realized how ridiculous it sounded. He could see no reason why a xenoborg would be bothering with such small game when there was plenty of larger and more nourishing sustenance to be had.

"That's not a fish," O-33 contributed. "It looks like a silver-colored lily pad." Then she moved to where she could get a wider view of the scene and added, "Dozens of silver-colored lily pads!"

"If those are lily pads, they're not from this planet," P-17 whispered skeptically as he came up behind her. "The last I heard, ours were green!"

The four Cyborg Commandos had been on a routine scouting mission in the Kettle Moraine area in southeastern Wisconsin when they had come across this seemingly solitary xenoborg. They could have killed it on sight, but they quickly realized that something unusual was happening — because xenoborgs were almost never known to travel alone. So the Cyborg Commandos decided instead to lay low and simply keep the creature under surveillance.

The xenoborg, its eight spindly legs barely able to support its massive, bloated body, had waddled down to the rocky, deserted shoreline of a quiet stream. The terrain was so rough and overgrown that the CCs had a difficult time at first determining just what the creature was up to. W-105's remark about "fishing" was perhaps little better than a wild guess, but as the CCs looked on it began to seem as though he might have hit close to the truth.

Floating gently in a small pocket of water were many flat, silvery objects, some of them very difficult to see as the setting sun glinted off the surface of the water. With motions that were a combination of haste and delicate care, the xenoborg stretched out its tentacles, grabbed some of the objects one by one, and stuffed them into an opening in the side of its body.

"It's not eating them," observed S-24. He, like his companions, had seen xenoborgs consume food often enough — all too often, considering that most of the monsters' meals consisted of human beings.

"No," agreed P-17. "It's collecting them. But what *are* they?" He didn't expect, and didn't get, an answer to that question.

Cris Holman, the human being whose brain resided inside the body of Cyborg Commando P-17, found himself feeling curious and despondent at the same time. After spending more than two years as a CC battling the alien invaders known as xenoborgs, he thought he knew everything important there was to know about the creatures. He had thought that he and the other members of the Cyborg Commando Force were on the verge of turning the battle in their favor. But now, apparently, the xenoborgs had developed some kind of new resource. He didn't know what it was — and he was dying to find out — but he did know that if these shapeless silver things were useful to xenoborgs, then they were definitely harmful to the human race.

"We should have known," whispered O-33, echoing P-17's unvoiced thoughts. The brain inside that body belonged to Maura Woolsey. She loved Cris Holman, and she knew him better than anyone else on Earth. She was just as dedicated as he was to killing the xenoborgs or driving them off the planet, and just as disheartened to find out that the CCs and the rest of mankind had something new to contend with.

"I don't get it," said S-24 as he noticed the xenoborg do something else unexpected. The creature picked up one of the silver objects, seemed to examine it briefly, and then placed it back in the water. "Why take some of them but not all of them? If I live to be twenty-five, I'll never understand the xenoborg mentality." Tony Minelli, before he became Cyborg Commando S-24, had prided himself on being able to come up with a wisecrack for almost any situation — and that part of him had not changed when his brain had been transplanted into a cybernetic body.

"Our orders don't include trying to figure out how these things think," said W-105, the newest member of this CC team. "We don't have to understand, just observe and report." Richard Adams had only been a member of the CCF for about three months, but had taken to his new life quite readily. Unlike his three teammates, he had been a soldier before undergoing his brain transplant, and he remained a soldier after it. He didn't question orders; he obeyed them. He didn't ask for reasons, just assignments. He didn't worry about methods, just results.

In some ways Richard Adams reminded Cris, Tony, and Maura of John Edwards, their former partner, who had been killed in action several months ago. Richard had the same general outlook as John, who had also been a military man before his transplant operation. But while John had his fun-loving and humorously sarcastic side, Richard Adams tried to be all business. However, in the last few weeks since joining the team led by Cris, W-105 was becoming more and more "human." Now Richard occasionally made speculative remarks, like the one about fishing that he had voiced a short while earlier. Even though W-105 scolded himself afterward most of the time when he did such a thing, Cris was glad to hear him thinking out loud. Richard Adams was a good soldier and already a credit to the Cyborg Commando Force, but Cris thought he'd be an even better CC when he realized there was more to fighting xenoborgs than following orders and making reports.

About twenty minutes later the bulbous creature, apparently done with its task, turned away from the water and shuffled off in the direction opposite the place where the cyborgs remained hidden. It had picked up and carried off eighteen or twenty of the silver things, but had left about a dozen still floating in the inlet of the stream. After waiting for a few minutes to make sure that the xenoborg was out of sight, the four teammates cautiously left their hiding place and ventured toward the water. The things floating on its surface did not seem to notice, or if they did, they certainly didn't seem to care.

"Do you think they can see or hear us?" Tony asked, feeling more than a little apprehensive about this new, unknown variable.

"I don't think they're capable of that," Maura said, trying to sound reassuring even though she did not feel completely confident that the featureless disks floating in the water were harmless. "They look like some sort of weird vegetation," she ventured.

"Maybe they're a source of food or vitamins," Richard offered.

"Could be," Cris put in quickly, eager to be supportive of Richard's attempt to contribute. And he noticed, with pleasure, that W-105 did not follow this remark with some sort of negative reaction. "And if they are essential to the well-being of the xenoborgs, then it's certainly our duty to destroy them and any others we might find. But first, I want to get a closer look at one of them."

"Take your pick," said Tony, sweeping his arm toward the area where the things were clustered. "I'm not touching 'em. I'd rather just blow them out of the water."

"Be careful, Cris," said Maura.

"I'll cover you," said Richard, taking a position off to one side where he could get a clean shot at any or all of the unidentified floating objects.

"We'll all cover you," said Tony, moving to Cris's other flank while Maura began scanning the terrain they had just moved over.

Cris inched toward the shoreline, keeping his own arms in front of him, knuckles pointed out and ready to shoot laser beams at an instant's notice.

"If one of those things so much as quivers, blast it!" he ordered, never taking his eyes off the strange, floating blobs.

"Don't worry, pal!" S-24 answered with serious sincerity.

* * *

Tony wasn't using the word "pal" casually; in fact, he and Cris had been friends — close friends — since shortly after the aliens had descended on Earth. Tony had helped ease Cris through the days following the initial invasion after Cris's father, stepmother, and sister were murdered by xenoborgs. Cris had also thought that Maura was dead when he found her apartment building in Whitewater, Wisconsin, reduced to rubble, but a year later the two of them were reunited.

Cris discovered that at about the same time he was assuming she had died, she was viewing the wreckage of his own family's home twenty miles away outside the city of Delavan and thinking that the worst had happened to him. While she headed south to escape the monsters and try to build a new life for herself, Cris became fast friends with Tony and stayed in the southern Wisconsin area.

All three of the young people came to realize that mankind's best hope of beating back the alien onslaught was in the production of Cyborg Commandos — super-soldiers composed of human brains that were removed from their natural bodies and transplanted into computer-assisted cybernetic bodies. In three different places and at three different times, Cris, Tony, and Maura all underwent the transformation into CCs. Later Tony and Maura were transferred to the CC base in Manitowoc, Wisconsin, where Cris was stationed, and the three of them had been together on most of their missions ever since. They were bound together by more than a sense of duty and obligation, by more than the existence of a common enemy they all despised beyond words. Their bond was formed of mutual love and respect. Cris had known each of the other two before they had all become Cyborg Commandos. He had come to appreciate them and love them as human beings, and he thought of them as human beings still. The strongest incentive of all was that one day when this was all over, they would be able to become fully human again, able to enjoy and cherish each other the way friends and lovers were meant to.

The Higgins-Whitaker Brain Transplant Reversal Procedure would make that possible. Initially, those who volunteered to become Cyborg Commandos were taking an enormous risk above and beyond the dangers of the transplant operation or the threat of the invading aliens, because mankind had not developed a way to change a CC back into a human being. Each volunteer's body was placed in cryogenic storage and kept alive (medically speaking) in the expectation that the secrets of the reversal procedure could be unlocked — and finally they were.

The knowledge did not come without its price, and it was a heavy price indeed for Cris Holman. His natural mother, Nora Whitaker, literally worked herself to death in an effort to perfect the process. She succumbed to a massive heart attack just before the first successful transplant reversal was performed, and so was denied the joy of knowing that her son would be able to reoccupy his natural body. The process she had helped to devise bore her name along with that of her partner, Dr. Francis Higgins, and Cris appreciated that tribute despite the sadness he felt every time he heard the phrase "Higgins-Whitaker."

The discovery was important for reasons that went beyond the welfare of those who were already Cyborg Commandos. The Cyborg Commando Force had remained small in the first months following the invasion because most people weren't willing to take the chance of never being normal humans again. But now thousands of other men and women, secure in the knowledge that they could someday return to their normal bodies, volunteered to have their brains transplanted into cybernetic capsules.

As the CCF drastically increased in size, mankind's chances of eventually beating back the xenoborg invasion improved accordingly. But there were still hundreds of thousands of alien beings spread across the surface of the planet. Even the "ordinary" creatures were dangerous enough — gruesome, ruthless things weighing a few hundred pounds apiece. Using their tentacles, pincers, and sheer bulk, they could kill and devour human beings with ease, and several million people had already fallen prey to their rampaging.

Cyborg Commandos, equipped with built-in weaponry, defense mechanisms, and high-technology sensory devices, were more than a match for normal xenoborgs. But CCs couldn't just wade into alien strongholds and start blasting away — because a small percentage of the xenoborgs, apparently the leaders or officers in the invasion force, were similarly equipped with weapons and electronic aids — technological devices that they actually carried inside their bodies and somehow were able to use just as if the weapons and sensors were biological organs.

Everyone had come to realize that the key to eliminating the xenoborgs was destroying these leader-types, or at least rendering their weapons and sensors useless. But no one had figured out just how to accomplish that objective. Many more human lives were being lost every day; the world population had been cut by a third, and the planet, devastated from all of the brutal warfare, was in need of major rehabilitation before it would ever again be as beautiful and bountiful as it had been in the days prior to the invasion. At the moment, however, the only concern on the minds of the four CCs at the stream containing the foreign objects was whether or not those unknown factors were capable of doing them harm.

* * *

Cris stood on the edge of the shoreline for what seemed an eternity to his companions. Finally, satisfied that the floating disks were going to stay put, he slowly lowered his body into a squatting position. Then, keeping one laser-arm trained on the water, he reached down with his right hand and carefully touched the top of one of the objects of his curiosity.

"Yeow!" The cry of surprise came from Cris and Tony at the same time. In the same instant that Cris drew his hand back from the thing he had touched, Tony jumped aside as a small patch of ground next to him briefly sizzled and turned brown.

Maura whirled and rushed to Cris's side as he took a couple of steps away from the shoreline. "What happened?" she asked excitedly.

"I'm not sure. I think those things bite!" Cris said, staring at the water. "Only they have no teeth, so judging from the surge that went through my system just now, I'd say they're packing quite a charge."

"But if you're the one who touched the thing," said Tony petulantly, "why am I the one who almost got fried?" He was staring at the small patch of ground that looked as though it had been struck by a miniature lightning bolt.

"It happened pretty fast," said Cris, "but my guess is that the shock went along the surface of my body and then jumped to the nearest ground — which just happened to be the ground you were standing next to."

"Can't be," said Richard matter-of-factly. "They're just floating there. No wires, no power source—"

"Eels don't have wires, either," Tony said matter-of-factly.

"But these aren't—" Richard began to point out the obvious before Maura interrupted.

"They may have some of the same properties as eels," she said, "but they're certainly not part of the nematode family."

"What kind of toads?" Tony asked, not wanting to sound ignorant but unable to hide his curiosity.

Maura stifled her urge to giggle. "Nematode, Tony — as in elongate fishes."

"Oh, *that* kind," Tony said, hoping he sounded like he knew what she had been talking about.

"Whatever they are, they seem to have electrical components," Cris said seriously. "It's a good thing for me my coaxial shielding and insulation were in good shape, or I'd be history."

"So what do you think they're for? They can't move on their own — or at least don't seem to want to," Tony said.

"They certainly aren't hostile," Maura said, thinking out loud but not choosing her last word too carefully.

"Easy for you to say — you didn't touch one!" Cris said indignantly.

"What I meant," said Maura with a bit of an edge in her voice, "was that they didn't attack you — you attacked one of them, and maybe it was just defending itself."

"But that xenoborg who was fishing them out of the water didn't seem to get zapped," Richard said.

"No, it didn't," Cris said thoughtfully, and then added, "Either the xenoborg knows how to handle them to keep from getting shocked, or they know how to keep their charge from going off when a xenoborg touches one of them."

"I don't think they *know* anything," ventured Tony. "They're machines or devices of some sort, not organisms."

"A machine with no moving parts?" asked Maura. "How do you explain that?"

"Not a machine," said Cris before Tony could get out a retort. "More like a battery."

"Yeah!" said Tony, glancing at Maura as though he had been vindicated. "That's what I meant."

"That could be right," Richard said. "But why are we standing here trying to figure it out? We should get back to the base and let the scientists take it from here." His tone was slightly condescending, as was usually the case when he felt it necessary to point out something that his companions should have thought of already.

"You're right, of course," Cris said, mildly irritated by Richard's tone and adopting his I'm-the-one-in-charge attitude in response to it. "You and Tony report back. Maura and I will stay here for a few more hours, keep an eye on the place, and see what happens."

"We're not supposed to split up," Richard pointed out.

"Technically, corporal, the general order prohibits one of us from going off without the others. It doesn't prevent me from splitting this four-member group into a pair of two-member teams for a good reason. And this is a good reason."

"Maybe another xenoborg will come back to pick some of these things up or drop others off, and we can learn something more about them," Maura suggested, hoping to ease the tension between Cris and Richard before it got worse.

"Among other things, I want to know why the xenoborg took some of the things and left these others," Cris said. "I want to know how a xenoborg can touch them without getting zapped. I want—"

"I want to get out of here before one of those things decides to take another electrical potshot at me," Tony interrupted.

There was silence for a moment. Then, in an even, inoffensive tone, Richard said, "You don't have to explain yourself, sir. I'll report what we've found out and wait for you to follow us back. How long will you stay here? Shall we say six hours?"

"Maybe six, maybe sixteen, maybe more. If I don't know anything about what I'm trying to do, how can I predict how long it will take?"

"Yes, sir. Just concerned about the lieutenant's safety." The statement was delivered in a clipped, military style, but Cris could hear the genuine feeling beneath it.

"I appreciate that, Richard, but don't worry."

"Not worried, sir. Just concerned."

"Let's hit the road, one-oh-five," said Tony. "Believe me, the lieutenant can take care of himself. See you soon, Cris. And Maura, don't let him do anything I wouldn't do."

Maura chuckled. "And what wouldn't you do?" she asked.

"For one thing," he said, "I wouldn't take off my shoes and go wading. For another thing—"

"*Go*, Sergeant S-24," said Cris, pointing imperiously in the general direction of Manitowoc.

When Richard and Tony were out of earshot, Maura rested her hand on Cris's arm and said, "Richard really seems to get to you."

"Oh?" Cris said, feigning surprise. "It shows?"

"Oh, a little bit, yup," Maura said, her tone light and teasing.

"I know," Cris said, his voice taking on a more serious tone. "But I just don't know how to deal with Richard sometimes. He's a real enigma. He acts like he's one of the group, and then he acts like a soldier, and then he switches back again."

"You change moods, too."

"He doesn't change moods — he changes personalities. I never know which Richard I'm going to come up against."

"Maybe part of the problem is that you're subconsciously comparing him to another soldier we both knew and loved," Maura said tenderly.

"Maybe not even subconsciously," Cris admitted both to himself and Maura at the same time.

"I miss John, too," Maura said softly. "But we can't blame Richard for his death. It must be hard for him to step into a slot left open by someone the three of us loved so dearly. Richard must feel like an outcast, considering how we're always pointing out that if John was here—"

"Oh, Maura . . . If John *was* here, he could tell me how to handle situations like this, instead of me having to give orders to some stranger I don't even like!"

"Give him a chance, Cris. He's not bad, he's just not John. No one will ever be able to take John's place, but from what I can tell already, Richard Adams has all the makings of a superb soldier. Let's try to appreciate him for what he is, instead of what he's not," Maura urged gently.

"I can try," Cris said after a pause. "But there's one thing I'll never get used to."

"Which is?"

"I wish he'd stop calling me 'sir' — I hate that!"

Maura giggled. "I admit it doesn't seem to fit. But it *is* a very definite sign of respect. And anyway, we all call you 'sir' sometimes."

"Yeah, but when he says it, he *means* it."

Maura laughed again and then added playfully, "Wait til he gets to know you better, sweetheart. He'll treat you with as little respect as the rest of us do."

"Just wait til you get your real body back. I'm going to tickle you till your teeth fall out," Cris growled threateningly.

"Oh yeah?" Maura challenged. "Well, that's nothing compared to what I intend to do to you, buster!"

Cris felt a mental surge of warmth. "You know, when you talk like that I could almost swear I still had some parts they claim to have removed when I became a cyborg."

"I know what you mean," Maura sighed. "But, alas, I do believe it's just wishful thinking."

"That, and one hell of a good memory!"

Maura was about to respond when a very familiar and unpleasant sound brought an end to any further reminiscing.

2

March 17, 2037

It had never admired anyone or anything else before. Respect was something It reserved only for Itself. But now, feeling confident and somewhat magnanimous, It found Itself paying a silent tribute to the inhabitants of planet Earth. For more than two of this world's years, It had been watching mankind struggle to regain control of the world it had once dominated. This species was one of indomitable spirit. It had never seen the likes of such before.

In spite of that unsettling bit of data, however, It was not overly disturbed. They were strong fighters, but all they were doing was delaying the inevitable. Its pawns, the xenoborgs, had done well. By force of numbers and with the help of the Master's technological brilliance, they had eliminated a sizable segment of the human race. And even though the xenoborgs had also sustained considerable losses, they still continued to fight for dominance in a world they would never possess, for they had no idea, and never would know, what they were fighting for. Their victory would be Its victory.

Although It would have ordinarily enjoyed the challenge that this world presented, It was becoming more and more preoccupied with a feeling of vengeance. It had developed a philosophy to suit the situation, an outlook that fit well with Its view of the universe around It. When one encounters an enemy worthy of respect, it becomes all the more important to humiliate and destroy that enemy.

The humans had upset Its plans in a way It had not anticipated. It was furious at the idea of having been made the fool. But It also knew that Its emotions had to be kept under control. If It allowed Itself to become unnerved and permitted others to see that reaction, the loss of self-respect would be devastating. It had to stay calm and resolved and finish Its task. But inwardly, with a fervor that went far beyond Its usual detachment, It would savor every moment of mankind's collapse.

The evil creature rolled Its bulbous head from side to side, a gesture that indicated It knew It was still in control. Each of Its three suckerlike mouths smacked in unison, almost as though taunting Its enemies, although the foes could not — and never would — come into contact with It.

It coiled Its slimy, wormlike body around the glowing, sticklike protrusion that served as Its home post, using most of Its eighteen small tentacles to pull Itself up and around the thing until the finished product resembled an indigo-and-silver-colored barber pole.

When It was comfortable, It cleared Its mind and set to work.

* * *

The lone xenoborg was not inclined to take on the enemies it had spotted. In the first place, the bloodless blob knew it could never win. These quasi-humans were too well protected, had too many weapons, and seemed to possess the technology they needed to have destroyed thousands of its alien comrades. For a long time, the xenoborgs had known all they needed to know: these super-soldiers with their inboard lasers, microwave projectors, and sonic vibrators were to be avoided — especially when they appeared in pairs or greater numbers. All the xenoborg really wanted to do right now was find one real, flesh-and-blood human and satisfy its hunger.

The creature turned and began moving away from the approaching cyborgs. The thing knew they had not seen it, so all it had to do was take a different path than the one the other group was traveling.

It ambled away very slowly, not wanting to attract attention, but had gone only a few dozen yards when it unexpectedly and inexplicably turned and maneuvered itself into a position behind the soldiers. Its desire to destroy one of the mechanical men was suddenly stronger than its will to live. The determined creature plodded along slowly, methodically, toward the fulfillment of its purpose. It didn't question the change in tactics; it didn't even notice there had been one.

The alien had a singleminded purpose — it didn't matter how that had come to be. What did matter was the death of its foes, the purpose for which this creature now lived and breathed — if not for very much longer. The objects of its hostility were now within its range of vision.

The obsessed xenoborg carefully extruded a pulser weapon from one of the craterlike openings in its body and aimed it at the cyborg that brought up the rear of the group. Almost instinctively, the soldier turned toward the creature, but in the same instant an explosive pellet was expelled from the pulser. The shot hit the enemy's body, blasting a jagged hole in one of its legs, and the cyborg was immobilized.

The xenoborg was fighting a battle it could not win, but it didn't know that and wouldn't have cared if it had been aware of the fact. Unmindful of its impending doom, the creature wasted no time in turning its weapon on another member of the squad. At the same instant that a projectile hit another one of the cyborgs, the soldier's two remaining squad members raised their arms, and a double burst of lasers cut the alien to pieces.

* * *

It didn't grieve for the loyal subject It had just sent to its death. Instead, it delighted in the success of the test. Never before had it been necessary to force xenoborgs to sacrifice their lives, to send them up against what they should have realized was certain death. It was confident that It had the mental power to compel these creatures to do such a thing, to override their instinct for self-preservation, but It could not be absolutely sure of that until It had experimented.

Two of the mechanical soldiers had been damaged, which was much more than It had hoped for. If that was the result of taking over a single creature and sending it to its death. . . .

It reveled at the prospect of how much destruction It could cause by dominating the minds of a great number of xenoborgs and directing them to attack with no regard for their own welfare. The xenoborgs existed to serve It — and if serving meant dying, then so be it. Planting the compulsion to die in all of its minions would take some time, but when the process was complete nothing would be able to resist the rampaging, suicidal hordes.

It convinced Itself that this latest change in tactics was all part of Its plan — a plan that It was exceedingly proud of. The xenoborgs had been specially crafted for the attack on this planet because It wanted to take advantage of man's inborn fear of one of the least dangerous but most numerous life forms on Earth — the insect. The attacking troops were made to resemble mites, a type of creature that was especially repugnant to humans, but were of course much larger, more horrible, and far more dangerous.

To prevent man's defenses from blunting the attack before it could really begin, the invasion force had been brought in under cover provided by turbulent weather, purposely caused by a supposed meteor shower that had triggered the detonation of a few dozen nuclear devices at the South Pole.

The attack force that assaulted the earth during the initial invasion descended upon that planet in huge armored creatures produced by the same sort of genetic engineering that had produced the xenoborgs. Hundreds of thousands of the alien warriors landed on Earth within a matter of hours on January 13, 2035. The aliens appeared on every major continent and within every political boundary. They set to work immediately destroying known military bases, missile silos, airport runways, and shipyards throughout the world.

Within days the planet was firmly in the grip of

the alien troops. Many of the major governments had collapsed. Between a quarter and a third of Earth's human population had been killed or injured, and most of the humans who survived the invasion had been forced into hiding. Confused and terror-stricken, many poeple hid in cellars, caves — anywhere the xenoborgs did not seem able or inclined to penetrate. Most modern conveniences were interrupted. Food and water distribution, power and light, and communication became things of the past in many areas of the world.

It loved moments of reminiscence. It loved to dwell on Its own brilliance. Now, thinking back across hundreds of Earth years, the Master remembered the time the decision had been made to add this planet to Its roster of conquered worlds.

Sometime around the early part of Earth's 13th century, It had landed an automated probe on Earth's moon. And the things It had learned from this probe intrigued It. It wanted this planet — and what It wanted, It got.

The probe that It relied on for monitoring and analyzing the development of human civilization had transmitted a large body of information to It in the Earth year 1922. It had instantly grasped the realization that this was not an ordinary planet and that *Homo sapiens* was not an ordinary sentient life form.

Mankind had made remarkable progress between the 13th and 20th centuries. The pace of man's technological development exceeded that of most civilizations It knew about, although man's was one of the youngest. The probe observed and reported the results of man's rapid development, but what it did not and could not convey was the principal reason for this ascendancy — the human spirit.

It knew that man liked to think of himself as aggressive, inquisitive, eager to explore new frontiers and improve his lot, but It paid this attitude little heed. It had learned through long experience that all sentient races liked to think of themselves — indeed, *had* to think of themselves — as questers after knowledge, seekers of the unattained. But It had proven, time and time again, that this self-importance was a fallacy, a delusion perpetrated upon themselves by those who could not bear to think of themselves as inferior to a higher form of life.

It did not entertain the possibility that, for once, a sentient race might actually possess the qualities it attributed to itself. But It did realize that It should not let any more time pass before devising and implementing a plan to take Earth. If It waited any longer, man's steadily improving technology would make the conquest time-consuming and troublesome. So It began to plan and plot, still feeling no urgency, and brought Its plan to fruition a little more than a century later.

A century was no time at all in Its frame of reference, but it was enough time for mankind to progress, technologically and psychologically, to a point where the race was actually capable of putting up a fight to save its home world. If It had programmed the probe to report several decades earlier, if It had been in a position to strike in 1922, man could not have withstood the assault. But by the year 2035, things were different.

None of this occurred to It, of course. Its perspective remained unchanged. It was a member of the Master race, beings who felt quite justified in calling themselves the Controllers of Reality. And reality in Its terms amounted to subjugation, destruction, and domination — control over every habitable planet in the universe.

It would be impossible for man to conceive, much less understand, the mentality of the Controllers. There was no class struggle in Its civilization; there had never been a war with others of Its own kind. The concept behind Its civilization was one that, if it could be acknowledged at all by a lesser life form, could only be believed and accepted. And to accept was to die, because nothing could stand in the way of Its supremacy.

Mankind was proving difficult to convince. The Master could tell that the human race still found it hard to believe that its existence was coming to an end. So, the Master had begun searching Its mind for other ways to make the outcome evident, ways to break man's spirit.

And Its latest touch of inspiration would no doubt accomplish just that. Until now, the Master had been allowing the xenoborgs to act "intelligently," permitting them to be driven by twin desires of triumph and self-preservation. But if those desires conflicted with each other, if the former could not be achieved while the other existed — as seemed to be the case now on planet Earth — then all It had to do was command Its minions to stop being concerned with self-preservation, to consider survival no longer a goal.

Triumph was all that mattered. The cost was not important. If It had to sacrifice every xenoborg in order to achieve victory, then It would do exactly that. And if It had to turn planet Earth into a lifeless sphere of rock at the same time, then that too was justifiable. It would have preferred to save the planet for future use — but more than anything else, now It had to *win.*

3

March 17, 2037

They stood shoulder to shoulder, their fear acting as an adhesive that kept them in place, barely allowing themselves to breathe for fear of being discovered. The frightened group of misplaced humans had been closet-bound for nearly forty-five minutes. They had been cooped up too long now, and Dan was worried that the baby would wake up and start crying any minute. If he did, there was little hope of their survival.

An unexpected and certainly unwanted guest had upset the day's plans for the newly formed family when the creature had shown up in the yard of the abandoned country schoolhouse they called home. The visitor, one of the alien insects, rummaged through everything in its path, apparently looking for something good to eat. Those crouched in silent terror inside the janitor's closet of the former school knew exactly what it was looking for. They had seen groups of similar creatures devour family members, friends, and scores of other humans. And there had been times when each of them had barely escaped becoming nourishment for the creatures.

Dan shifted his weight slightly from one foot to the other. The quarters they had chosen as their hiding place were cramped at best. The cobweb-covered walls formed a four-by-six foot space, just enough room to contain the eight people who sought refuge behind a somewhat battered old oak door. Breathable air was not a problem, thanks to a small opening near the ceiling that led into the adjacent bathroom. But they had only a little space to spare; they couldn't all shift positions at once, and now Dan was beginning to feel the physical strain of holding the same uncomfortable pose for a long period of time.

The sudden, sharp sound of breaking glass startled those in hiding, including the infant, who until that point had been sleeping comfortably against his mother's shoulder. The baby stiffened and then began to fuss quietly. "Shhh, Jacob. It's all right," his mother Suzie softly cooed, gently rocking him and patting his back at the same time. Her husband Jerry, who was standing next to his wife and child, reached down and began rubbing the baby's still-soft head of blond peach fuzz.

"Maybe you should try nursing him," Jerry suggested, and as he turned toward her he realized that Suzie had already begun fumbling with the buttons on her blouse. She unfastened the garment with one hand because she didn't want to take a chance on handing the baby over to someone else; the shift from one person to the other might have really caused an uproar if Jacob decided he didn't want to leave his mother's presence.

Now ready to receive the squirming infant, Suzie shifted the baby from one arm to the other and guided his mouth to her breast. The child made a couple of sweeping motions with his head, his mouth playing back and forth across the nipple as though he was having a hard time finding it. As his lips formed a suction cup and grabbed hold of their target, his eyes rolled upward and he began hungrily sucking what little milk his mother had to offer.

Jacob Peters had been born in the rundown school building nearly three weeks earlier. His parents had used the structure as a place of refuge after driving from their last temporary home in Kansas City, Missouri, trying all the while to keep one step ahead of the alien creatures. They had been taking back roads and were uncertain as to their exact location when they came upon what used to be Shadow Lawn School near Delavan, Wisconsin. At the time the building had been deserted, and the area surrounding it appeared to be free of xenoborgs. Since Suzie was within days of delivering the baby, the couple decided their best bet would be to set up temporary housekeeping inside the building. The old schoolhouse seemed an ideal place to hide. Stuck out in the middle of cornfields, and looking as though it had already been ravaged by scavenging monsters, it seemed unlikely the creatures would bother with it.

The school building did not have a basement, but the gymnasium was in the very center of the building, and the big room had no windows to give the outside world a glimpse of the kerosene lanterns they used to see by at night. Jerry and Suzie had spent the first peaceful week of their recent lives in that gymnasium. They had been on the run, in and out of abandoned houses, warehouses, grocery stores, and barns since the aliens had landed more than two years ago. It was nice to have some respite from the terror. And when Jacob was born a week after they arrived at Shadow Lawn it had seemed, for a while at least, like they were the only three people in the entire world.

They had come to the school with enough food to last them several weeks. Their latest supplies had come from the basement shelves of an abandoned farmhouse. Whoever it had belonged to had been long gone by the time Jerry and Suzie had arrived there, and although it had bothered them to simply take the food, there seemed to be no reason to let it go to waste. There was good cause for them to believe that whoever had lived in the warm, country home would never return to consume the remaining jars of canned vegetables and fruit.

The family's quiet little world had been abruptly disturbed about a week after Jacob's uncomplicated birth. The three family members had all been sleeping on one of the torn blue wrestling mats that had been left behind when the school had closed. Jerry had figured the time to be well after midnight when he heard footsteps and voices directly outside the gymnasium. He quickly awakened Suzie and pulled her and Jacob into the janitor's closet that stood to the right of the boy's locker room.

They had waited there, holding their breath, while the intruders tried to push their way in through the locked double doors leading to the gymnasium. When they apparently decided that no amount of force was going to budge the heavy steel doors, the owners of the muffled voices moved away. Jerry and Suzie had listened in fear as they heard the group circling the gym, trying the two remaining points of entrance.

Now, as Jerry and Suzie again hid inside the small, dark room, the events of that tense time came back to their memories. Jerry allowed himself a small smile as he thought about the irony of it. The last time we were here, he thought, there was plenty of room for the three of us. But now, pressed all around them were the same people they had been hiding from that night.

"It's getting quiet. Maybe the thing's finally moving on." Karen's cautious whisper was barely audible.

"Does that mean we can go out now, daddy?" Ryan asked his father, his small-voiced whisper full of hope.

"No, guy. I'm afraid we'll have to wait. The creature may still be out there, even though it doesn't seem to be trying to tear into the building any more," Dan answered his eight-year-old son, his tone apologetic. He spent a lot of time these days apologizing to Ryan, in one way or another. Silently apologizing for having brought him into this world that had become so horror-filled; for not having been able to save the boy's mother a year ago when the aliens had discovered the family hiding inside an old barn; for not having the nerve at that time to turn the rifle that had provided absolutely no defense against the creatures on his only child and thus spare him any more pain and suffering; for continually having to be on the run; for dozens of other tragedies his son had lived through over which Dan Murphy had no control.

Karen Sullivan knew how Dan was feeling, even when she didn't know he was feeling it. She had been in that barn when Dan's wife had been ripped to shreds. The woman's agonized screams had sent shock waves surging through her entire body.

Although Karen's husband had also been killed during the same attack, his death, at least, had been much swifter and less painful. And Tom Sullivan was not someone his wife would ever grieve for anyway.

Tom had been physically and verbally abusive to his wife during much of the four years of their marriage. And even though the couple had not lived together during the last two years of that relationship, Tom had continued to harass Karen, even going so far as to assault her in the street outside her apartment. The only reason the couple was together in the barn where Tom Sullivan and Sharon Murphy lost their lives was because Tom had been on his way to pay Karen one of his unwelcome visits in the early morning hours when the invasion took place. And when he insisted she leave her home in Milwaukee, which had been hard hit by the aliens, she had not argued.

Together they had moved around the area for a few weeks, never staying in one place long, in an effort to hide from the monstrous creatures. They ended up on the outskirts of the small town of Mukwonago, where they had joined a group of other terrified humans who were hiding out in an old barn, hoping the whole, unbelievable nightmare would soon be over.

It wasn't.

Karen shuddered inwardly as she tried to force the memories back down, tried to get her mind off the awful sights and sounds that had punctuated the last two-plus years of her life.

"This wouldn't be half as bad if we had some decent music to listen to, y'know?" A voice beside Karen abruptly halted her morbid thoughts. Karen gave the lanky, sixteen-year-old, pimple-faced boy standing beside her a sympathetic glance. He and his grandmother had been through as much as anyone else in that room — maybe more.

"Is that the only thing you can think about at a time like this?" the old woman on the other side of the boy whispered tersely.

"No, but it's better than anything else that comes to mind," the boy answered snidely.

"Shhh!" was the woman's only response.

Kirk Christiansen shrugged. He was used to his grandmother's cranky nature. He had never much liked her, but she was the only family he had left now. He took a deep breath and stifled the urge to cry. He hated even thinking about the reason he was stuck inside this room with his father's disagreeable mother and a group of strangers. He couldn't easily deal with the tragic turn his life had taken in the last two years. He couldn't face the week of horror he had been forced to live through a little more than a month ago. He didn't dare dwell on his mother's pitiful cries or the sound his dog's bones had made as they were crushed when one of the horrible creatures had walked over the animal after knocking it unconscious. He couldn't stand the mental image of his father being torn to shreds and then eaten by the monstrous bugs.

Despite his best efforts to keep his mind on anything else, those grisly scenes played over and over again in his head for most of his waking hours. And he knew there was only one way he could ever get them to stop. Kirk fully intended to get free of this hellish life as soon as he got up the courage to end it for himself. He felt more and more strongly all the time that there was no reason for him to continue living in a world that held no hope or future for him.

Anita Christiansen often wondered what was going through her grandson's mind. Until the invasion, he had been a self-centered, ill-mannered, tobacco-chewing slob. She hated to think of her own flesh and blood that way, but reality was reality, and she couldn't deny what kind of a person Kirk Christiansen was. Where he had gotten his personality, she would never know. Her own son, Edward, was a responsible, caring human being, as was his wife, Sonya. And they had raised the boy with all the love, support, and affection any child could need. Maybe they had been a little too giving, the woman thought as she stood in the dark room, wishing she didn't feel so much older than her seventy-three years.

She had been living with her son and his family when the invasion took place. She had been there for about a month while recovering from cataract surgery. And, although she had enjoyed spending time with Edward and Sonya, her grandson's laziness and constant lack of regard for anyone except himself continually upset her.

The boy seemed to have nothing going for him except for his appreciation of bad music. Anita had found it very difficult to live with the constant unsettling dissonance produced by his highly amplified collection of so-called music provided by the latest and loudest popular groups.

It was true that she hadn't had much use for the boy. But now that his parents were dead, she felt that it was her responsibility to stay with him and care for him. And after all he'd been through, she did feel sorry for her grandson. The terrible events that he had witnessed had changed Kirk in a way Anita couldn't quite figure out. Of course he was affected — who wouldn't be? But he almost seemed as though he was trying to act like he didn't care about what was going on around him; like he was resigned to living with things the way they were.

"I think we've waited long enough. There hasn't been a sound out there for some time now." Dan's observation interrupted Anita's thoughts. "I'm going to go out and take a look around," Dan announced, still talking in a quiet tone of voice.

"I'll go with you," Jerry offered.

"Me too," Karen added.

"I don't think all of us should go. One person

can move around more quietly than two or three. And if that thing's still out there, one can get back a lot faster than two or three," Dan said.

"Then let me go," Karen volunteered. "I can do what needs to be done."

"No," Dan responded. "I should go because I'm the only one here who knows how to use a gun."

"A lot of good that'll do you against one of those things!" Jerry said.

"Well, it's better than trying to use my hands," Dan countered and then quickly added, "And I promise I'll be very careful."

"I don't want you to go, Daddy," Ryan said, his tone full of pleading.

"I'll be all right, guy. And once I see that the coast is clear, we can all get out of this little room and celebrate by opening a few bottles of that soda pop we've been stashing away for so long now," Dan said, trying to cover his apprehension.

"How long should we wait once you leave?" Karen asked.

"Don't leave here until I come back and let you know that it's safe," Dan responded.

"And if you don't come back? Then what? Do we just sit in here until we rot?" Kirk asked, his tone almost challenging.

"I *will* be back." Dan's tone was full of angry determination. He was annoyed at the boy for asking a question that could only instill more fear in his young son.

"Oh, come on! How can you be sure of anything? Do you really think you're going to get a chance to guzzle that stupid soda pop? What kind of a celebration is that, anyway?" Kirk retorted cynically, the corners of his mouth turned slightly up in a cruel sneer.

Jerry Peters broke into the exchange before Dan could respond. "Look, son," he began, trying to be patient and understanding. "All of us are aware of the dangers we face, but negative attitudes aren't going to get us anywhere. So why not just relax and look forward to getting out of this closet?" Jerry felt sorry for the kid. He had seen the look of despair in Kirk's eyes growing more pronounced every day. And he could easily relate. He had to deal with his own feelings of hopelessness on a daily basis, and he failed more often than not, so how could he expect someone half his age to take his advice?

Kirk shrugged his shoulders and said nothing. The way he saw it, the only thing any of them had to look forward to was more of the same, up until the moment one of those ugly creatures chowed down on them. And the way he felt right now, he'd almost prefer it if that happened in the next five minutes.

Dan gave his son an affectionate pat on the head. "You do what these people tell you until I get back. Okay, guy?" he asked, his tone much lighter than his heart. "I'll be back before you know it."

"I hope so," Ryan said weakly, not at all convinced.

"He'll be okay. I'll see to that," Karen said, putting one arm around the child and giving Dan a look that she hoped would convey to him that, if necessary, she would "see to that" as long as she was alive.

Dan gave her a quick, appreciative glance and then squeezed his way to the door of the tiny room. He turned the knob and very slowly pushed the door open a crack. There was nothing out of the ordinary in his line of vision. He pushed the door open a little farther and, satisfied that there were no aliens in the immediate vicinity, he eased the door open wide enough to fit his tall, muscular frame through and then quickly shut it behind him.

Dan peered around the corner into the main part of the gymnasium. From all appearances, nothing had disturbed the group's living quarters. He walked into the gymnasium and, keeping close to the wall, inched his way toward the nearest exit, his rifle cocked. When he reached the exit, he became aware of his heart beating hard inside his chest. All sense of bravado gone, he wondered what it was like to be eaten alive. He shuddered as he remembered how his wife had screamed for what seemed like a long time before finally, mercifully succumbing.

His palms were sweating badly now as he reached for the lever that would release the bolt on the left side of the heavy steel doors. He pulled down on the lever and the lock gave way, making a sharp clanking noise in the process. Dan's heart nearly stopped, and he held back, his sweating hand still pressed against the door handle. If there was an alien on the other side of that door, the noise would have alerted it to the fact that someone was about to come through.

Dan stood there, afraid to move one way or the other. When a full ten minutes had gone by without the slightest sound coming from the other side of the steel barrier, he pushed the door open and peered out. Again, there was nothing in his line of vision.

"Coast is clear, or at least the hallway is," Dan whispered quietly to himself, as though verbalizing the absence of danger would make him more convinced that it was so.

He tried to reassure himself, as he moved out into the narrow hallway, that if something was close by inside the building, it would have showed itself by now.

The hall was lined with windows, most of them broken. Dan shuddered when he thought about how close the intruder, or perhaps intruders, had been to the frightened humans hiding in the janitor's closet. If the thing had been able to get inside the building through the broken window, there was no evidence of such a thing having happened. And he knew nothing had attempted to get inside the gymnasium, or they would certainly have heard it from their hiding place.

Dan turned to his right and walked down another hallway, this one lined with classrooms. He stole a quick look inside each room and continued on down the hall. He remembered the first time he had made his way around this school. . . .

* * *

He had insisted on leaving Ryan, Kirk, and Anita sitting in the car while he and Karen checked out the inside of the seemingly abandoned building. They had checked out every classroom, every office, every restroom. But when they had tried to get inside the gymnasium, they had come up against locked doors at every entrance.

At first Dan had thought that a group of xenoborgs might be camped out there, but when he really thought about it he couldn't imagine why the monstrous creatures would want or need to lock the doors. Cyborg Commandos could blast right through the steel with their lasers, and any humans who might walk in would be welcomed with open tentacles.

The two quickly made the assumption that there must be at least one scared human being hiding behind the locked gymnasium doors. But it could be dangerous, nevertheless, to walk in unannounced. If whoever was in there was armed and thought he was being threatened, that person could fire first and ask questions after the fact. Dan had seen that attitude many times in the last few months — men and women who in better times would not harm a flea, but who had been turned into selfish, vicious scavengers because that was the only way they could survive. He had felt that way himself more than once, but thankfully had not become vicious himself . . . at least not yet.

If he and Karen were wrong, and for some reason a group of — or even one of — the gruesome aliens was behind those doors, then they wouldn't have a chance in hell of getting out of there alive. Nor would any of those waiting for them outside in the car.

Dan and Karen had split up briefly while they were scouting around the outside of the big room, and on her excursion Karen discovered a cold-air return vent that was large enough for her to fit through. She took off the cover and crawled along the passageway, which as she suspected opened into the gymnasium.

After satisfying herself that the room was empty, Karen moved around the perimeter and gave the bathrooms a quick check, opening the door to each one and quietly asking, "Is anyone there?"

The men's room was adjacent to the closet where Jerry and his family were hiding. When Jerry heard Karen's voice through the wall separating the two rooms, he decided to take a chance.

He asked in a low voice, "Who is it?" When she heard the question, Karen almost cried from relief.

She ran the few paces from the bathroom doorway to the door of the closet and tried to talk through the crack between the door and the frame. "Don't be afraid," she said trying to sound calm and soothing even though she was probably as nervous as the man inside. "There are five of us out here, just looking for a place to hide and rest. We won't hurt you or take any of your food." She heard the sound of a lock being turned and then stepped back as the door opened slightly. Karen Sullivan smiled, and Jerry Peters smiled back. The eight of them had been together ever since.

* * *

A door leading to the playground stood at the end of the hall. There were no windows, so Dan went into the last room on the right-hand side and looked out the windows of what was once the first-grade classroom. The playground appeared to be deserted, and the windows in this particular room were unbroken. Dan decided to backtrack his way to the front of the structure and, once there, looked out through the large, glass doors. The only thing he saw for as far as his line of vision would allow were stark, abandoned corn fields and an old, run-down farmhouse.

Dan took a deep breath and pushed open the

front door of the schoolhouse, half expecting a large tentacle to reach out and coil itself around his body. He stepped through the doorway into the sunlit yard and took a deep breath. So far, so good.

It took Dan about ten minutes to walk around the outside of the small structure, keeping himself as close to the brick walls as he could manage. He came to a complete stop each time he reached one of the six corners, venturing a very cautious peek around the edge before resuming his slow pace. There was no sign of life anywhere in the schoolyard.

But there were other signs, and they served to verify what he already suspected.

The yard was strewn with debris, as though something had been conducting a search. "Must have been looking for food," Dan muttered as he walked through the messy yard. Mounds of earth had been torn up in places, exposing the black, rocky soil that had been covered by grass earlier that day. The tattered remains of a small animal of some sort, Dan couldn't tell what, lay off to the side of one of the toppled swing sets. Bits and pieces of broken glass lined the outside of the building, and old desks rested in topsy-turvy fashion, some on their sides and some on their backs, as though someone had reached in through the hole where the window had been and had pulled them out and thrown them around.

At least one of those things has definitely been here, Dan thought. But it was gone now. And he, Ryan, and their new "family" were still alive.

"Count your blessings," Dan muttered cynically as he completed his circuit and prepared to head back inside. He was within a few feet of the front door of the building when something he saw out of the corner of his right eye caught his attention. Dan turned quickly and took a good look. Perched on top of a hill, about three hundred yards away from where he stood, were four of the monsters.

And they were looking right at him.

4

March 17, 2037

"Get down!" Cris said in a loud whisper. Even before he uttered the words, Maura was throwing her body flat against the gradual incline next to the stream.

Cris followed suit, orienting himself to face the direction the sound was coming from. There was no mistaking what it was — the same unearthly noise he had heard practically every day since becoming a Cyborg Commando.

He listened, trying to gauge the distance and velocity of the creatures making the sound. It was the characteristic shuffling, thumping, rustling noise of xenoborgs dragging their bulky bodies over the ground. Any large Earth animal would make noise moving through underbrush, but this sound was different. It had a heavy, almost wet, quality, and it seemed sinister. The characteristics that made this noise distinctive were impossible to put into words that someone else could understand, but the sound was one that every Cyborg Commando quickly learned to identify.

After a short time, he realized that the sound was coming toward them at an angle but the creatures were still a considerable distance away, far enough from them that he and Maura didn't have to worry about being detected, at least for the moment. "Let's get some cover," he said in a low voice, gesturing toward a thick cluster of bushes about thirty yards away from where they were.

They got to their feet and, in a crouching run, covered the intervening distance in a few seconds. They settled down behind the first row of bushes, squatting so they couldn't be easily seen behind the five-foot-high shrubbery.

Cris's instincts took over briefly, and he thought about moving to another hiding place on the other side of the creatures' apparent path so that he and Maura could catch them in a crossfire as they approached. He was about to announce his intention to do that when he remembered the reason they had stayed behind. Their purpose was to observe and gather information, not to go wading into a battle.

And, as had been happening more and more often lately, Maura seemed to be right in tune with his thoughts. "It looks like we're going to get our chance to do some fact-finding," she said. "They're heading this way."

"Okay," Cris said. "Be ready to defend yourself, but don't shoot unless they see us."

"Yes, *sir*," she answered, putting a bit of unnecessary emphasis on the second word and touching his arm to let him know she was being humorous, not sarcastic. She knew that a little levity helped defuse the tension of a situation, and Cris almost always took it the right way.

"Sorry," he said. "I guess you already knew what to do, didn't you? Sometimes my 'orders' are a little obvious."

"A little," she said with mock disgust. Then her voice took on a light tone again. "You just keep on telling me what to do, dear. That way if anything goes wrong, I can blame it on you."

"Ah, the things we officers are forced to put up with—"

Cris broke off his response and the two of them froze as the noise suddenly increased in volume. His first thought was that the xenoborgs had somehow covered a couple of hundred yards in the blink of an eye and were now almost on top of them. That was wrong, of course. The creatures had not abruptly come closer, but the sounds of their activity were much louder. And now the noise was more than the sounds of movement. Mixed in with the shuffling and thumping were crushing, crunching, tearing sounds — the noises of destruction.

"What's going on?" asked Maura, surprise and concern evident in her tone. Cris didn't bother to respond with an "I don't know"; instead, he concentrated on getting a new fix on the noise.

Fortunately, the monsters had not changed direction. They were still on a route that, if it was maintained, would cause them to pass within about fifty yards of where Cris and Maura were hiding. And they had not increased their speed; if anything, they were moving more slowly than before.

The more Cris thought about every aspect of what was happening, the less sense it made to him. Xenoborgs characteristically did not move through uninhabited areas at night; yet it was late dusk, almost dark, now, and a small group of creatures was certainly on the march a short distance away.

When the monsters had to move at night, they generally did so with as much caution as they could manage, whenever possible staying on open, flat ground where the shuffling, rustling sounds of their passage would be minimized. But when he and Maura first detected the presence of this group, they were forcing their way over rough terrain and apparently not caring about the noise they made as they bent back tree branches and trampled the leafless underbrush.

Now they were not only moving over the rough terrain but seemingly trying to cause as much commotion as they could in the process. Cris heard an occasional splintering crack that he assumed was the sound of a thick branch or a small tree being snapped in two. He heard the sounds and felt the vibrations of large, heavy objects — boulders or fallen trees, he supposed — being cast aside, hitting the ground, and bouncing or rolling before coming to a stop. If these creatures were trying to attract attention, they were doing a very good job of it.

And he couldn't forget about the most mystifying aspect of this whole adventure — the disclike, silvery things that were still floating unobtrusively on the water behind them and to their left. The xenoborgs in the distance were traveling parallel to the stream, not toward it, so it didn't seem as though they were interested in the silver things. But how could he know? The monsters could change direction at any time. Maybe they would hold their course until it brought them to the point of closest proximity to the silver things, and then they would make a sudden right-angle turn toward the stream — heading right for the place where he and Maura were crouching.

The chance of them bring trapped between the xenoborgs and the electrified silver things was slim, but Cris wanted to reduce it to zero. "Come on," he said, breaking the silence. "We gotta get out of here."

Maura started to protest. "But if they see us—"

"Either they'll run the other way or we'll blast

them," said Cris as he sprang to his feet, realizing even as he said it how simplistic that response was. He had left out an important third possibility: If one or more of the approaching xenoborgs was equipped with weapons and sensing devices, and Cris and Maura got themselves into a vulnerable position, they might be lucky to escape with their lives.

Although she had her doubts about relinquishing their hiding place and moving away from where they could keep an eye on the silver things, Maura had no immediate opportunity to discuss the decision. Cris grabbed her wrist, pulled her up beside him, and started to head away from the stream.

They ran haltingly, darting from shrub to shrub and tree to tree. "We're cutting right across their path!" Maura said, a little panicky because she wondered if Cris had somehow lost track of where they were.

"All the more reason to hurry," he said in a self-assured tone. "Don't worry — if we can't see them yet, then they can't see us either." As long as the CCs used only voice communication and didn't switch on their radios or their own sensory devices, they didn't have to worry about being detected from a distance by a xenoborg that might have its own sensing equipment. And the two groups were still too far apart for visual contact, especially in the severely rolling terrain of the Kettle Moraine area.

When they were about a hundred yards away

from their first hiding place, and that much farther from the stream, Cris spotted an enormous fallen tree, its partially decayed trunk about four feet in diameter. "Over there," he said, pointing. Both of them vaulted over the log and settled down in prone positions behind it, facing the place where, Cris estimated, the xenoborgs would be coming into view in another three or four minutes.

Because of a small, steep hill that crested about fifty yards to the west of where they were hidden, Cris and Maura didn't get a glimpse of the monsters until the sound of their approach had increased to an almost unbelievable level. Although they still instinctively communicated in whispers, the CCs could have talked in loud voices without being overheard by the xenoborgs. The noise level was so high that sometimes their whispers were drowned out even though Cris and Maura were only a few feet apart.

"They're on a rampage," Cris said softly. "But for what? There are no people around here."

"Maybe they're just mad," Maura offered.

"Is there such a thing as a good xenoborg?" Cris shot back.

"No — I said 'mad,' not bad." Despite the tension mounting inside her, Maura chuckled.

"You'll have to speak up," Cris said sternly to cover his embarrassment, speaking at normal volume. "I can hardly hear myself talk, let alone . . ." He stopped, realizing that the noise level had suddenly abated. Now all they could hear was the usual sound of xenoborgs plodding along, without the crunching and cracking and smashing noises that had been filling the air for the last several minutes. The creatures were just on the other side of the crest of the hill, and Cris quickly realized why the sounds of destruction had trailed off. Most of the top of the hill was devoid of vegetation except for ground cover. The xenoborgs were still moving, but at the moment they were moving over ground that didn't have any features they could crush, smash, or trample.

Then they came into view almost simultaneously at the top of the hill: six xenoborgs traveling abreast, each one fifteen or twenty feet away from its neighbor. This, too, was unusual; xenoborgs moving in a group were almost always encountered in single-file formation. They shuffled forward in unison, as though they were puppets all being controlled by the same strings. Each one would move a few feet forward, then pause and swing the front section of its bulbous body from side to side, scouring the ground in an arc in front of itself, looking like nothing so much as a ghastly organic vacuum cleaner. When all of them had finished their sweeps of the areas they were responsible for, the entire group would waddle forward another few feet, and the "cleaning" motion would resume.

There wasn't much they could crush or trample on the ground they were moving over, but that didn't keep them from giving it their best try. Occasionally one of them would dig in with a pair of pincers and uproot a patch of grass. Any vegetation more than a few inches high was surrounded by a tentacle and either uprooted or ripped to shreds. The whole exercise seemed methodical and at the same time mindless. The xenoborgs were obviously heedless of what might be going on around them, of who might be watching. They seemed only to care, quite literally, about what was happening right in front of their noses.

Noiselessly, Maura inched closer to Cris. "I've never seen anything like this," she said. "What's the point?"

"Maybe there is no point," Cris speculated. "Or maybe . . ." He let the rest of the thought go unvoiced, as though by not saying it he could keep it from coming true. "Let's see what happens when they hit that patch of shrubbery," he added before Maura could prompt him to finish his earlier statement.

The line moved inexorably down the hill until, at the edge of the downslope, four of the xenoborgs ran into the bushes Cris had referred to. Suddenly, those four began to act like creatures possessed. As soon as they felt the perimeter of the patch of shrubs with their tentacles, they started to move more vigorously . . . more viciously. They raised the front parts of their massive bodies a few feet into the air and lunged forward, bringing their bulk down on the three-foot-high bushes. They twisted to one side and then the other, grabbing and pulling and rending, flattening or tearing up every bit of vegetation of any appreciable size. As they moved on through the patch, they left behind them nothing but dead or mangled vegetation and torn-up earth.

Very infrequently, one of the monsters would grab a few branches or a clump of roots and shove them into what passed for its mouth cavity. They could eat vegetation of all sorts — as far as anyone knew, they could use anything organic for nourishment — but this was clearly not a foraging expedition. This was a mission of destruction.

"My God . . ." Maura breathed. She was not awed by what the xenoborgs were doing — she had seen them wreak much greater destruction than this — but by the way in which they were going about it. For no apparent reason and with no apparent goal in mind other than the destruction itself, these six monsters were cutting a hundred-foot-wide swath of devastation through what had once been a beautiful woodland wilderness. If six could do this much damage, what about sixty? Or six hundred? Or . . .

"Are you thinking what I'm thinking?" Cris whispered.

"I'm afraid so. Cris, what if those things are changing their tactics? What if they're suddenly hell-bent on—"

Cris didn't allow her to finish. "As Richard would

say, that's a question for the scientists. Let's just sit tight and see what happens next." He had a strong temptation to stand up, shout, and wave his arms at the advancing line, just to find out for sure that they were oblivious to his presence. But he didn't. None of the monsters were brandishing any weapons, but he had no way of knowing if they were packing lasers or some other death-dealing devices inside their bodies. The awful fact was that they didn't need technological weapons to do what they were doing right now; the sheer power of their bodies and extremities was enough.

About two minutes later the monsters were on a direct line between the CCs and the place in the stream where the silver things had been floating. If they're going to head for the water, Cris thought, now's when they'll make their turn. He wasn't surprised when they stayed on their straight-ahead course, but what he saw a few seconds later shocked him into speechlessness.

Xenoborgs, despite their limited reasoning ability, had always had a healthy respect for objects bigger or stronger than themselves. They knew enough to go around a big tree or circumvent a patch of dense woodland rather than try to knock over the tree or force their way between several trees that grew close together.

Until now.

As the line moved forward, one of the xenoborgs in the center of the formation came upon a modest-sized maple tree. The thing moved toward the tree until its snout was touching the trunk. Then it reared up especially high, as though proud of its discovery, and threw its body forward with all the force that its bulk and its back legs could provide. The body hit the tree about eight feet above the ground with a soft, solid thud, and the tree visibly bent under the creature's weight and the force of the blow. Once more the xenoborg threw the front of its body up into the air and came hurtling down. This time the trunk splintered where the monster's body hit it, sending a sickening cracking sound through the night air. When the creature pulled back, the tree remained bent at an ugly, unnatural angle.

The xenoborgs on either side of the tree-smasher had finished gouging the areas in front of them by now, and while the other monsters waited in place these two moved in to help finish what their comrade had started. One of them began ripping up the ground at the base of the tree while the tree-smasher and the other one flanked the dying maple, raised the fronts of their bodies, and extended their tentacles. They gripped the tree above where the trunk had begun to splinter and then pulled themselves up until their bodies were almost perpendicular to the ground.

With around a half-ton of weight pulling out and down, putting stress on its already fractured trunk, the tree didn't have a chance. Slowly at first, then with increasing speed and a rapid series of cracking, splintering noises, the trunk gave way and the top of the tree plummeted to the floor of the forest.

That could have been sufficient — should have been, Cris thought — but the xenoborgs weren't done yet. Four of them attacked the upper branches of the fallen tree, breaking the smaller pieces of wood and gouging the larger ones, while the fifth one moved to assist the monster that had continued to rip at the ground around the base of the tree. The two of them exposed several of the large roots that fed directly into the trunk and then scratched and pulled and gouged at those roots, occasionally pulling at or slamming into the broken-off trunk as though they were trying to rip it entirely out of the ground.

Time passed very slowly for Cris and Maura during the four or five minutes after the top of the tree came crashing down. It seemed to take forever for the xenoborgs to finish their systematic demolition. In an effort to keep from being overcome by emotion, Cris tried to rationalize, to define, what he was seeing. All of the devastation the xenoborgs had wrought since the invasion was senseless from the human point of view, but at least he could imagine some purpose behind what the creatures had been doing. As much as it sickened him to think of all the lives that had been lost, all of the trappings of men that had been destroyed, he could at least understand that sort of destruction. It was like war, where killing people and wrecking things was a means to an end.

He knew he was capable of killing; that had been proven many, many times over during his career as a Cyborg Commando. But his killing and destruction were directed against an enemy that was trying to do the same thing to him. His actions, like those of the xenoborgs, had a purpose that went beyond death for death's sake. Clearly, they wanted to conquer and possess the planet of man. Just as clearly, man wanted to prevent that from happening.

But the maple tree and the woodland around it were no one's enemy. And these creatures were definitely making sure that it was not only damaged, but that no part of it would ever grow again. There was only one purpose Cris could imagine for why xenoborgs would cast all other concerns aside in favor of this singleminded, wanton ruination of the world itself. And, just as the first time the thought had occurred to him, he pushed it out of his mind and refused to verbalize it. He tried to force himself to hope that what he was seeing was merely an isolated incident of pointless destruction, but the analytical and pessimistic side of his personality just couldn't see it that way.

"What if they did that to everything they came in contact with? How would we ever rebuild?" Maura asked softly as the xenoborgs moved onward. She was not expecting an answer. Cris heard more than her words; the emotion behind them spoke even louder. He knew she was searching within herself for a way to deal with what had just happened. Cris wanted to protect her, to reassure her, to dissuade her from thinking the things they were both thinking. If six of them could do this much damage . . .

"What was the point, Cris?" she asked plaintively when the xenoborgs had moved farther away, still chopping and grinding and crushing anything in their path.

Again, it was the kind of question that didn't require an answer, but Cris saw in it an opportunity to make both of them feel a bit better. "No point at all, as far as I can see," he replied, trying his best to believe his own words. "Just six monsters doing a little hell-raising. Who knows, maybe even xenoborgs need to let loose once in a while." As soon as he said it, he knew he had gone too far with his last remark.

Maura turned to face him, taking her eyes off the monsters for the first time since they had come into view. "I don't know how much of this 'letting loose' we can take," she said, dead serious.

"Wanna go after them?" he asked in an upbeat tone, hoping his mood didn't seem as artificial as it was.

"Too risky. If just one of them is armed—"

"I know. But . . ."

"And I know what you were going to say. 'But if

we let them go, they'll keep on rampaging until someone does stop them.' Am I right?"

As if on cue, the noise coming from their left abruptly dropped off again. Just as before, all Cris and Maura heard now were the telltale sounds of xenoborgs clumsily making their way along the ground. The monsters were still in sight, and Cris could see that they were in an area of thick undergrowth. But now they were acting like "normal" xenoborgs again. They plodded and shuffled over the terrain, compressing or trampling small vegetation in the process of moving but no longer making a concerted effort to kill everything before them.

Neither of the Cyborg Commandos said anything for several minutes, and finally Maura broke the silence as the monsters moved out of sight down a steep incline. "I guess they're definitely done," she said.

"Yeah," Cris said absently, resisting the urge to add "for the time being."

Maura sensed the distress he was trying to conceal, and now it was her turn to get his mind off the recent events. She did it with a remark she knew would get to him. "Let's go back to the water and wait till sunrise. If nothing happens by then, I say we head for home."

"Hey!" Cris said with feigned irritation. "Who shorted out and left you in charge, anyway?"

"Sorry, sir. What are your orders?"

"Well, I'd say we should go back to the water

and wait till sunrise. If nothing happens by then, we head for home."

"Whatever you say, sir."

They got up from behind the fallen tree and, hand in hand, walked back the way they had come. When they had to step over the ground the xenoborgs had ravaged, Cris forced himself not to look down.

5

March 18, 2037

At Tony's insistence the two Cyborg Commandos went directly to Traynor's office upon returning to the Manitowoc base in mid-afternoon. Tony said he was too anxious to report their findings to take the time to go through the regular routine of recharging their primary batteries and then waiting to be contacted for a status report.

Richard knew this was a contravention of procedure, and he wasn't comfortable about it, but he could tell Tony was not to be dissuaded. He did try to get Tony to stop long enough to send a short message to Traynor, alerting the man that they were on the way, but S-24 never broke his stride.

"Sorry, sir, but we need to talk to you," Tony blurted out as he unceremoniously pushed open the door to Traynor's office.

"You're back earlier than we expected. Is something wrong, Tony?" Traynor asked the anxious cyborg. Not one to stand on ceremony, Traynor was not especially irritated about the two CCs bursting into his office. He was, however, concerned that they wouldn't have used such an approach if they didn't feel an urgent need to see him. "Where are Maura and Cris?" Traynor asked, watching the open doorway for some sign of the other two squad members.

"They're still in the field, keeping their eyes on some UFOs we discovered down by Rice Lake."

"UFOs?" Traynor asked, obviously puzzled and somewhat alarmed.

"Yeah. Unidentified Floating Objects. Some kind of electrically charged lily pads!" Tony confirmed.

"Okay, Minelli. If this is another one of your practical jokes or a product of your weird sense of humor, I have better things—"

"No sir, he's not joking!" Richard broke in, and then added, "He's just a little overexcited. You see, we—"

His impatience getting the best of him, Tony interrupted his teammate before Richard had a chance to finish his explanation. "We discovered some strange sort of xenoborg sidekicks while patrolling the Kettle Moraine area."

Traynor gave the two cyborgs a hard, penetrating look and then nodded his head toward two empty chairs in a gesture indicating that they should both sit down. "Okay, I'll bite, although God knows I'll probably regret it," Traynor said and then, in a tone of resignation, he added, "So tell me about these so-called water lilies — and please, Tony, speak English!"

Tony and Richard spent the next fifteen minutes taking turns relating the events leading up to the discovery of the electrically charged disks. While they talked Traynor listened attentively, the thumb and forefinger of his right hand pulling the corners of his bottom lip together until they touched in the middle. He was hardly aware of this gesture, although anyone who spent any time with the man knew this nervous habit as one of his trademarks.

When they were finished, Traynor said quietly, "We know a little bit about the alien life form I think you and your teammates have stumbled across. But I wasn't aware that they were carried around inside the xenoborgs' bodies. And we had no idea there were any located in this area."

"So, what are they? What do they do?" Tony asked.

"We don't know much, I'm afraid," Traynor answered. "They play some sort of role in the invasion, but we don't know how important a role that is.

"We know they're living organisms, but they don't attack unless provoked. We know they can really screw up a CC's electrical system if they're touched, and some of them can kill a human being on contact. Some are more harmful than others, depending on how much power they contain."

"You mean like how many volts are running through it?" Richard asked.

"Something like that. Only these things aren't connected to any power station. They're like real powerful batteries — batteries that can soak up and spit out a whole lot of power."

"Wow! I wish I'd known about these things when I was spending megabucks on batteries for my sonic jacket," Tony said, his mind wandering back to the time when, as a high-school student, he had worn the contraption almost all the time. A descendant of the large, portable cassette players and radios that were enormously popular in the late 20th century, the "jacket" resembled a wide belt with attached suspenders and contained two sets of speakers, a battery compartment, and a miniature compact disk player. For about two years after he got his, about the only time Tony removed the apparatus was when he took a shower or went swimming.

"But what is their purpose, sir?" Richard asked politely, but not before throwing a lingering glance toward Tony. W-105 was obviously disgruntled at S-24's cavalier attitude, and Tony picked up on the mood instantly.

"Sorry for the digression," Tony said, being facetious. "I have a tendency toward association. It helps me to understand something if I can relate it to a personal experience. Now if you were to say the word—"

"Excuse me, sergeant, but I find your attitude more than a little baffling," Richard Adams said, his tone holding a hint of controlled anger.

"How so, corporal?" Tony asked, stressing the last word.

"Your friends are risking their lives in order to get more information about these potential killers you jokingly refer to as 'UFOs.' We're here trying to conduct an impromptu briefing — impromptu because you insisted it be, rather than following procedure — and I'm getting fed up with your happy-go-lucky approach toward almost anything you come up against. This is a serious situation. How about a little respect for the position we're in?"

Before Traynor could intervene, Tony was on his feet. "Listen, corporal! I have all the respect in the world for people who deserve it, Traynor here included. But I don't have any respect for people like you who walk around oozing doom and gloom. I'd like to take that chip off your shoulder and put it—"

"That's enough, sergeant," Traynor interrupted in an icy, no-nonsense tone.

"I'm sorry, sir," Tony said dejectedly. "It's just that the corporal doesn't seem to know how to laugh. I wouldn't be surprised if his real face had a frown frozen in place!"

"Sergeant S-24! This is the last time I'm going to

tell you. Knock it off — now!" Traynor's voice was raised several levels higher than usual as he issued the firm command.

"Yes, sir," Tony said, a little sheepishly.

"Look, gentlemen, we seem to have a personality difference here. And the CCF doesn't have time for such things. So before this goes any farther, why don't I put in a request for a new fourth partner for your team, Tony? And Richard, I'll assure you placement with another top-rated group of soldiers. Agreed?"

"Fine by me!" Tony said eagerly.

"No," Richard contributed, his voice low but firm.

"Corporal, why wouldn't you want to get out of what appears to be a hostile situation?" Traynor asked kindly.

"Because, sir, it would take time to make the switch — valuable time none of us can afford at this point. I'm a soldier first, sir, and it's my job to deal with hostility — even if it comes from my own teammates." The room was quiet for a few seconds before Richard spoke again, this time addressing Tony, his voice trembling slightly as he voiced his feelings. "Do you think I haven't noticed how you and your friends can barely stand having me in your presence? To his credit, Lieutenant P-17 at least tries to be civil. But I know that every time he looks at me he's reminded of the teammate you all lost. He's even slipped and called me 'John' a few times. And when he does, he mutters an apology and then gives me this hateful look like it's my fault that your friend is dead.

"I can't help what happened to C-12. And I'm getting a little tired of trying to fit your mold. I'm not John Edwards. I never will be. Whatever it was about him that turned you all on, I don't have it.

"But I'm here to help stop too many others like him from losing their lives to these hideous beings. I'm here to help rid this world of these aliens who have the mistaken impression that this planet is theirs for the taking. And I'll die before I'll give up and let them have their way!"

Tony listened attentively while Richard talked. And when he responded, it was with barely controlled emotion. "Look, man, we weren't trying to make you feel like an outcast. It's just that you're so serious, and John, well, he used to have a way of making light of a difficult situation, which made the rest of us feel a whole lot better. And I have a habit . . . I try to laugh off a lot of things that I have a hard time handling. I figure the way things are these days, if you don't have a sense of humor, you'll go crazy!" Tony's voice changed as he spoke until, by the time he was finished, it had reached a high, emotional pitch.

"You both have good arguments, of course," Traynor said, his tone compassionate. "But some kinds of personalities just don't mix. For your sake, Corporal Adams, I still suggest that you at least consider a transfer."

"No, sir," Richard said stubbornly. "Order me to change units if you want to, but otherwise I'll stay where I am. One interloper is as good, or bad, as any other. These jokers aren't going to accept anyone as a full-time partner until they get over the death of their friend."

"Jokers? Jokers?!" Tony laughed scornfully. "Just who does the corporal think he is?"

Richard's answer was delivered so quickly it seemed instinctive, almost mechanical. "A soldier, sir!" Again he had reverted to his crisp, military tone, which sharply contrasted with the flavor of his previous remarks.

Tony regretted this latest turn in the conversation. For one thing, he had no immediate comeback to Richard's response. For another, despite his objection to Richard's choice of the word "jokers," Tony thought to himself that he really did like Richard better when the corporal lapsed out of soldier jargon and reacted like a . . . a real person. And Tony was a little angry at himself for asking a question that brought Richard back into "military mode."

Traynor ended the brief silence with another attempt to establish control. "I know this is an emotional situation, gentlemen, but you're *both* soldiers and I strongly suggest that you both start acting like it. In fact, consider that an order!"

"Yessir," Tony mumbled.

"Yes, sir!" Richard's response was crisp, clear,

and automatic. They both say the same two words, thought Traynor, but the way they say them shows just how different they are. He still thought the ultimate solution was to split W-105 away from the rest of his group, but he couldn't bring himself to order the transfer. Instead, he decided to hold out hope that things would get better. After all, he reasoned, Cyborg Commandos were not exactly ordinary soldiers, and this would not be the first time that they were handled with out-of-the-ordinary measures.

"Okay, look," Traynor began, his voice calm again. "We've never fought a war like this one before, and we've never had soldiers like the Cyborg Commando Force before. Your emotions are understandably out of whack, and I sympathize with that. If I went by the book, I could have both of you broken down to Floorscrubber Second Class for what you've done and said since you got back to base.

"But today's military leadership, at least as far as I'm concerned, has to make allowances for circumstances. In light of that, Sergeant Minelli and Corporal Adams, I will ignore some of the highly unprofessional comments you have made here today. But you have to learn to work together — and I mean fast! You won't get a third chance. Understood?"

"Yessir,"

"Yes, sir!"

"Okay. I want the two of you to spend the next few hours, or however long it takes the rest of your team to show up, getting recharged, checked out, and making your official reports. As soon as Cris and Maura return, we'll find out if they learned anything new, and I'll schedule a full team briefing before you get your next assignment. Now get out of here," he finished in a softer tone of voice.

Tony and Richard left the room quietly, each ashamed of his behavior. Their rooms were located in the same section of the base living quarters, so they walked in that direction together.

"Look, I'm—" Richard began.

"Hey, guy, I—" Tony's words came on top of what Richard was about to say. Tony laughed. "Now you have to admit *that* was funny," he said, hoping to get a positive response.

"I'm sorry, sir. I just—"

Tony stopped walking and turned toward Richard, forcing him to halt. "Please! If you don't do anything else to help save this troubled relationship, at least stop saying 'sir.' Cris would tell you the same thing — neither one of us can stand it. It puts up a barrier that we're not used to. Don't you see?" Tony pleaded.

"I'm sorry, s— I mean, Tony. I was just going to say that it's hard for me to see any humor in anything these days. I haven't felt like laughing since — well, for a very long time now. If you don't mind, and I mean no offense by this, I'd rather you saved your jokes for someone who might appreciate them."

Tony didn't say anything to that, but continued to stand in front of his teammate and look at him for a few seconds. Although it was impossible to interpret the cyborg's expressionless face, Tony had read plenty into what the man had said — and what he didn't say. He thought back to a time not that long ago when he had first met another person who didn't appreciate his jokes, either . . . a young man named Cris Holman. And he remembered why Cris couldn't laugh.

The two of them started walking again and went the rest of the way in silence until they arrived at Tony's door. Then, before Richard could take his leave, Tony stopped him with an abrupt question.

"Since what?"

"Excuse me?" Richard responded, obviously confused.

"You said you haven't felt like laughing since . . . something belongs on the end of that sentence. You didn't say since what." Although he was unaccustomed to coaxing information out of people this way, Tony tried to prod gently, hoping Richard would take the cue and open up.

"I don't mean to be rude, but I really don't want to talk about it." Richard's cool, determined tone left no doubt that he considered the subject closed.

"Okay, pal. I'll try to respect your need to grieve privately — or whatever it is you're doing inside that brain capsule. But listen: If you have something heavy you need to tell someone, or if you just feel the need to vent your spleen for some reason, I make as good a listener as I do an aggravating goof-off."

"I appreciate the gesture," Richard said quietly. "Now, will you please excuse me?"

"Sure," Tony said. He stood in the corridor and watched as Richard walked another twenty feet to his door and disappeared inside his room. Then he spoke under his breath, addressing the teammate he couldn't see with words that he figured Richard wouldn't appreciate at the moment.

"It was much more than a gesture, Richard. And I think you'll come around — just like Cris did." Then Tony said a few words to himself, silently vowing to learn to tolerate his new teammate — and not just because Traynor had ordered it to be so. "I'll get along with him if it kills me!" S-24 told himself, making the words sound as though they were delivered through clenched teeth. Then he entered his room for what would turn out to be his last chance to take it easy for a very long time.

6

March 18, 2037

When Dan was finally able to look back on what had happened a day earlier, he realized that there was no way he could have prevented the chain of events that led to Anita's death.

But for a long while, he blamed himself. Just as he had blamed himself for the death of his wife. Just as he would blame himself when the next person he had come to know was brutally slaughtered while he stood by helplessly and watched.

That was the nature of the world in which he now lived. A world he barely recognized.

* * *

It didn't take Dan long to figure out that the building where he and his friends were hiding was now, at the very least, under surveillance by the hideous creatures they were trying to escape. "Damn!" he exclaimed loudly as he hurled his body through the door of the schoolhouse and took off in the direction of the gymnasium. "Damn! Damn!" The loud curses were all he could bring himself to say as he set off in panic to warn those hiding in the janitor's closet.

Jerry, who had decided that Dan had taken too long to come back and had ventured out as far as the west hallway, was the first to hear him coming. Jerry's heart began to beat furiously as he stood almost frozen in place. "Dan, is that you?" Jerry called out softly, fearfully.

"Jerry! They're out there!" Dan exclaimed as he came into sight around the corner of the hallway running perpendicular to the one where Jerry now stood, his fear almost overwhelming him when Dan suddenly turned the corner.

"Oh, thank God!" Jerry said upon seeing his friend. "I didn't know who was—"

"Didn't you hear me?" Dan asked, grabbing the man by the shoulders. "They're out there, and they know we're in here. They *saw* me, for God's sake! We've got to get out of here."

Dan grabbed hold of Jerry's arm and pulled the startled man back into the gymnasium. It took just a few seconds for Jerry to begin moving on his own. He grabbed Dan and stopped him just short of the door leading to the janitor's closet.

"Look, we can't get out of here. If we go out there, we'll just be playing into their hands," he whispered frantically, the fear inside him growing at the prospect of walking out the door into the tentacled grasp of one of the monsters.

"They *know* we're in here!" Dan argued, almost becoming irrational. "If we stay, they'll tear the building apart looking for us."

"But what else can we do?" Jerry asked, despair creeping into his voice.

"We can run for it. We can use both cars. We'll just have to hope we can outrun them if they decide to follow."

"It'll be hard to outrun anything with a fuel tank that's just about empty," Jerry said weakly.

Dan was silent for a moment, trying to deal with the anger that was welling up inside him. In his excitement he had forgotten about the fact that Jerry's car was low on fuel. He now remembered the man mentioning it once when the group was discussing various possible means of escape, most of which included the use of two cars. Jerry had said then that he should take a container and scout around at some of the area farms for a source of fuel. But that was about as far as the discussion had gotten, and now there was no time to solve the problem.

"We'll just have to take one car," Dan said and added, as if by way of reassuring himself, "We have no choice."

"There's no way all of us will fit in your little four-seater," Jerry argued.

"We'll have to," Dan said, his voice calmer now. "And we don't have any time to waste." With that he pulled open the door of the janitor's closet, where six people waited, unaware that before the end of that day their number would be reduced by one.

* * *

They rode silently, the only sound in the car made by Kirk's muffled sobs. Dan drove, while Suzie, Jacob, and Ryan shared the passenger seat next to him. Jerry, Karen, and Kirk filled the back, Kirk purposely sandwiched between Jerry and Karen for his own protection.

Anita's gruesome death had been the final straw for the troubled young man. There was no telling what he might do now. And the adults who made it their job to watch him were taking no chances.

Karen had given up trying to comfort the boy several miles earlier. "I killed her! I killed her!" was his only response when she tried to convince him that his grandmother's death had not been his fault. If Dan had any energy, he would have debated the issue, pointing out that *he* was the one who was within a few feet of the monster's tentacles; that the only reason Anita was dead instead of him was because he was younger, and by virtue of that, faster. Dan cursed himself silently, telling himself that if he had had an ounce of courage, he might have tried to distract the monster and give the woman a chance to get away. And maybe he would have escaped, too. With Kirk's help, Dan thought, the two of them might have been able to fight off the creature. Now, he'd never know for sure.

About the only thing Dan did know at the moment was that an old woman was dead because he had been too busy saving his own skin to notice that she had needed help — until it was too late to make any difference.

* * *

Dan led the group down a north-south hallway, past the now-empty principal's office; past the small library where unoccupied bookshelves still stood at attention along three of the four walls, as though expecting to be filled momentarily.

The group brushed against lockers and paint-chipped walls of the narrow corridor, their sense of urgency accentuated by the sound of glass breaking on the opposite end of the building.

"Hurry!" Dan commanded, and then held back and frantically urged the others to go on. The sounds of destruction were getting louder, but they had only a short distance to go to safety.

That was when Dan noticed Kirk's absence.

When the group had left the gymnasium, after grabbing very few possessions, Dan had led the way with Ryan, Suzie, Jacob, and Jerry close behind. Karen had come next, holding onto Anita's arm, the older woman huffing and puffing beside her. Kirk had brought up the rear. But Kirk was not in line now.

Dan cursed softly to himself, thinking the boy had stupidly gone back to the gymnasium to get something.

"Wait!" he shouted, causing the others to stop and turn around. "When was the last time any of you saw Kirk?" he asked.

"Kirk!" Anita cried, her voice filled with alarm.

"I thought he was behind us all along," Karen said.

"Damn!" Dan swore, and then quickly regained his composure. He reached into the pocket of his trousers and extracted a key ring. He tossed the keys to Jerry and said, "All of you go on ahead and get in the car. I'm going to go back and light a fire under Kirk. Watch for us to come out the door and then start the engine, unless any of those creatures start to bear down on you. In that case, get the hell out of here as fast as you can!"

"Not without you, Daddy," Ryan said firmly, the look in his eyes indicating that he'd rather take his chances with the monsters than leave his father behind.

"We'll catch up with you. Jerry, toss me your car keys," Dan ordered, and Jerry complied without question, sensing what Dan had in mind even before he spoke the words. "You pull as far down Mound Road as you have to, until you're able to get clear of them. Then wait. Kirk and I will take your car and meet you. There's certainly enough fuel left in it to go several miles."

"There should be, pal. Just be careful." With that Jerry took Ryan's hand and began moving down the hallway. The boy hurried along at Jerry's side, but he kept glancing over his shoulder at his father. Dan winked and gave him the thumbs-up sign, hoping to indicate that all would be well.

The only person who wouldn't follow Dan's instructions was Anita. "Come on, Anita, we have to hurry," Karen urged. But the woman refused to budge.

"I'm not leaving without my grandson," she said stubbornly, and added, "and no amount of prompting is going to change my mind."

Dan quickly decided to give in. There was no time to argue, and it made no sense to have someone physically force the old woman into leaving; that would only endanger yet another person's life. "Hurry, Karen. Go with the others. I'll take Anita with me," he said.

Karen, after a long glance backward, turned and began running to catch up with the group. "Come on," Dan said rather sharply as he took Anita's arm and hurried her along the corridor, back the same way they had just come.

The sound of breaking glass and other noises of destruction echoed through the hallways as Dan and Anita made their way back to the gymnasium. When they reached the door, they both stopped simultaneously, momentarily stunned by what they saw within.

Sitting at the bottom of a row of bleachers he must have pulled away from the wall was a very calm Kirk. He was not gathering possessions. He did not seem to be looking for anything or even seem to be concerned about the sounds in the hallway, sounds that were coming closer by the minute.

"What the hell are you doing?" Dan cried loudly, closing the distance between him and the boy in a few seconds. He grabbed hold of the boy's arm and tried to pull him to his feet. But Kirk's arm flared outward, breaking the man's hold.

"Leave me alone. I'm tired of this game, and I'm not playing any more. I don't give a damn who wins. I just want it to be over with."

Anita had come up behind Dan in time to hear her grandson's words. "Kirk, please. Don't argue with the man. We have to get out of here fast!" she pleaded urgently.

"You go, old woman. You don't have any more use for me than I do for you. So why stay and endanger your life?" Kirk asked angrily.

"Because you're my grandchild. Because in my own way, I love you," the woman responded strongly.

"Well, your idea of love sucks," the boy retorted, his eyes full of anger, hurt, and hatred.

"Come on, kid. We don't have time for a family feud. We have to get the hell out of here, and I mean now!" Dan said. He grabbed the boy again and this time forced him to his feet. "Now, damn it! You're coming if I have to drag you by the hair!"

Dan didn't have a chance to carry out the threat. He barely had the words out of his mouth when one of the monsters came crashing through the half-opened door, waving its tentacles around in front of itself.

The sight of the disgusting creature seemed to snap Kirk out of his suicidal mood, and he did not argue when Dan screamed, "Run! Out to the car — fast!"

Kirk took off, his instinct for self-preservation rekindled, leaving Dan and Anita several paces behind. Dan grabbed the old woman by the upper arm, so hard that she let out a cry of pain, and began half-leading her and half-dragging her across the big room in the direction of the door. She couldn't move quickly, but she was cooperating as well as she could.

Then Dan felt a force pulling Anita's body away from him. In the same instant that he looked over his shoulder, he instinctively released his grip on her arm — which probably saved his life.

Saved his life . . . but ended hers. Dan realized in the next instant that he should have positioned himself between Anita and the monster instead of pulling her along behind him. Maybe he could have held off the creature and fought his way across the gymnasium, keeping the alien from getting its tentacles on the old woman. If he had only thought about it. . . . If he had only cared as much for her survival as he cared for his own!

Kirk was halfway across the room when he heard his grandmother's screams take on a new intensity. He turned around in time to see the gruesome monster finish wrapping three of its tentacles around various parts of the elderly woman's frame.

"Nooo!" Kirk screamed as the alien began to tear the still-screaming woman apart.

Dan, realizing there was nothing he could do for her now, ran forward and threw a shoulder block into Kirk that propelled the youngster away from the monster. The impact seemed to reawaken something inside the boy, seemed to bring him back to some semblance of rationality once again.

But the rationality was fleeting. Kirk broke into a dead run, flailing his arms wildly and screaming and sobbing all the way, and even by running as fast as he could Dan was hard pressed to keep up with him.

They had escaped one monster, Dan thought as he shoved the boy into the car, but another one had been born inside both Kirk and himself at the same time.

* * *

He didn't remember how he had gotten here. Somehow he had moved from the gymnasium to the car and was now traveling north and east along a series of country roads.

All Kirk Christiansen knew was that he had killed her. And he would never forgive himself for that.

7

March 18, 2037

The rest of the night and early morning passed uneventfully for Cris and Maura, and each of them was even able to get about three hours of sleep — a respite from the real world that did a lot for Cris's frame of mind.

The parts of a Cyborg Commando that were electrical and mechanical didn't need to rest or be refreshed, aside from the standard recharging of the batteries that powered the body's weapons, sensors, and "muscles." But the biological part of a CC — the human brain packed into the torso of each body — could not remain conscious constantly and indefinitely. Sleep was as necessary to a CC as it was to a normal human being; every time a Cyborg Commando reported back to base, his or her between-missions schedule included an obligatory sleep period of at least four or five hours — no matter how urgently that CC might be needed in the field.

On extended missions, CCs were expected to catch rest when they could, to prevent brain fatigue from impairing their perception and judgment. In extreme circumstances a Cyborg Commando could tap into the supply of stimulants and antidepressants contained in each body, but few cyborgs Cris had ever known were inclined to take advantage of this "crutch." There was no substitute for real sleep.

He moaned softly as he began to regain consciousness. He felt the gentle pressure of Maura's hand on his left arm, then reached across his body and touched her fingers with his right hand.

"Sky's getting lighter," she said quietly. "Time to get back to work."

Cris pulled himself into a sitting position, and after a few more seconds to collect his thoughts he was fully alert. In the safety of his quarters he habitually took his sweet time waking up, but when he was outside he didn't allow himself that luxury.

"Status quo?" he asked.

"Nothing's changed," Maura answered. "Those things are just floating in place, and I haven't heard anything out of the ordinary since my watch started. Do you feel better?"

"Yeah, I think so," said Cris. "Seems like we've been here a long time."

"I know what you mean," Maura said. Reflexively, she glanced back toward the swath of torn-up ground the xenoborgs had traversed just a few hours earlier.

"How about we start heading for home?" Cris asked.

"Let's give it a little more time," Maura said after a moment of hesitation. "I have a feeling."

Cris had heard her use those words before, and he knew she didn't voice them lightly. The woman he loved seemed to have some innate but undefinable way of knowing, sometimes, when something significant was going to happen. She wasn't always right, but she had been right often enough to cause Cris to take her "feelings" seriously whenever they occurred.

"Tell me about it," he said softly.

"You know I'm not good at putting these things into words," she said a little edgily. He waited for her to continue, and after a few seconds she spoke again, the words coming haltingly.

"I've been staring at those . . . things . . . for the last three hours. I think they're . . . important, and I think it was lucky for us that we found them. I can't . . . I don't want to leave until we find out what's going to happen to them, and I think something is going to happen soon."

"How soon?"

"Don't *press* me, Cris. I don't know *how* soon. I just have a feeling. . . ." Her voice almost broke, and she turned away from his gaze briefly. Then she looked him in the eye again. "We've been through this before, Cris. You can either believe me or not believe me, and I won't be offended if you don't. I'm not that sure of it myself, so how can I complain if you decide not to take a chance on my 'feeling'? You're in charge, and—"

"I'm sorry, Maura," Cris interjected. "You're right — we have been through this before. If you think we should stay, we'll stay."

"Don't do it just to appease me," she said.

"I'm not."

"Then why?"

"Let's just say that I have a feeling about your feeling. You're not the only one around here who can play a hunch, you know."

* * *

The sun rose bright and warm; spring was coming early to this part of the northern hemisphere. As he and Maura sat and waited, relaxing but still on the alert for signs of any other life or activity, Cris enjoyed the warmth of the early morning rays against his body's artificial skin.

"Gonna be a warm one," he remarked idly.

"Yeah," Maura said. "Sure beats stomping around in snowdrifts, even with heating elements in your feet."

Cris swept his gaze across the silver things and

the surrounding area, once again noticing nothing different from the way the landscape looked the previous evening. Then he realized — something *was* different!

"Maura," he said. "Look at the water. What do you see?"

"The same thing you see," she responded without turning toward the stream. "The same thing we've both been looking at for hours now. What do you mean?"

"Look where the sun hits."

She pivoted and scanned the area again. The sun was a few degrees above the horizon and bright enough to illuminate the entire sky, but most of the rays coming from the eastern sky were interrupted or defused by the thick foliage around the stream. The only place getting a full, unimpeded dose of sunlight was the patch of water a few hundred square feet in the area right in front of them. The sunlight was glinting off the silver things, making some of them almost invisible because of the glare thrown off by their reflective surfaces. Now that she had noticed what made this little area special, Maura wondered how the difference could have escaped their notice for so long.

"I see," she said slowly. "But what could it mean?"

"I don't know yet," Cris said. "But I don't think it's a coincidence."

"Me neither. And I'm glad you noticed it."

"Credit where credit is due, sergeant. If it wasn't for your 'feeling,' we'd have been a few miles away from this place by now."

"Well, then, thanks to both of us, we now know something we didn't know before. Does that mean it's time to get going?"

"Not yet. So far we don't really know *what* we know. Let's give it another couple of hours."

"That's what I was hoping you'd say."

* * *

Three more hours passed, during which Cris and Maura engaged in a lot of idle conversation. But neither of them brought up the subject of whether, or when, to give up the surveillance and start back for Manitowoc.

Maura didn't want to say anything because something was still gnawing at the edge of her consciousness. Something else was going to happen at this spot, and she was afraid that if she talked about heading back, Cris would acquiesce and they'd miss their chance to figure out exactly what they had discovered.

Cris, likewise, didn't want to be responsible for ending the surveillance when, at any time, they might be mere minutes away from some new discovery. The feeling, he thought, was very similar to standing on a street corner and waiting for an electricab to happen by. You might wait for half an hour and not see one, but if you gave up and went to another intersection you'd never know if one did come by thirty seconds after you left. So, you stayed and you waited, telling yourself that you could afford another couple of minutes.

But it had to end sometime. He was responsible for their safe return, and he knew that even if they left for Manitowoc now, they would have been declared overdue for several hours by the time they got back. Regardless of how much information they came back with, he'd have a lot of explaining to do if he stretched this excursion out too much farther. . . .

With an audible sigh designed to help convey his genuine regret, Cris got to his feet and said, "We'd better get going."

"Okay," Maura said with an equal lack of enthusiasm. She also didn't like the idea of leaving, but she understood why they couldn't stretch it out any longer, and she wasn't about to complicate things for Cris by questioning his decision.

"At least we can shed a little more light on the subject," Cris joked.

"That's the kind of remark I would have expected from Tony," Maura said as she stood.

They headed to the northeast, quickly ascending the same hill from where the four team members had spied on the xenoborg last evening. Minutes later they were already almost two miles away from the spot where they had spent the night, on the fringe of a wooded area and about to move across a wide expanse of open ground.

Maura, scanning to the north and west while Cris watched the south and east, was the first one to spot the monsters.

"Cris!" she called in a soft voice. "Over there!"

He twisted in the direction she was pointing. A single xenoborg had just topped a small rise about a quarter-mile away. Because he and Maura were still in the grove of trees, Cris was positive the monster had not seen them. But its snout was facing directly toward them, indicating that it was traveling on a beeline for their exact location.

They kept low and watched for another thirty seconds. A second, and then a third, xenoborg appeared right behind the first one. Cris caught the reflection of sunlight off a couple of metallic objects located on the flank of the third one in line, and he immediately realized that this creature was packing some kind of weaponry — probably grenade launchers, judging from the location of the reflections off their bodies.

"Double back!" he called to Maura in a loud whisper. "Back to the water!" Both of them turned and quickly retraced the path they had just taken. When they reached the place where the silver things were floating, Cris took a brief look at the stream to be sure nothing had changed since they had left. The objects were still floating passively, still basking in bright sunlight.

They couldn't hide on the same slope they had used the night before, because if the xenoborgs were heading for this spot they would pass right over that hill. So Cris picked out a couple of places in a very rugged patch of ground slightly south and west of the stream. He motioned for Maura to take cover behind a boulder and tucked his own body into an enormous briar patch about thirty yards away from her. They wouldn't be able to communicate with each other as long as they held those positions, but at least they both had a good view of the small clearing on the shoreline next to where the silver things were floating.

The noise of their approach left no doubt in Cris's mind that the xenoborgs would pass very close to where he and Maura were hiding. But he knew they were well concealed, and if the monsters somehow did discover them, they could both hightail it over a nearby ridge and be out of sight in seconds. He was apprehensive as he waited, but not because he was worried for his or Maura's safety. He *wanted* the monsters to come close — he wanted them to come to the stream.

About fifteen minutes later, he got his wish. The xenoborgs — there were six of them altogether — trundled through the undergrowth, staying in single file as much as possible while veering to avoid trees and large growths of shrubbery. The one in the lead angled toward the meandering stream until it was about ten yards away from the water, then turned and began moving parallel to the bank. The others, naturally, followed suit.

When the first xenoborg spotted the silver things, it twisted its snout back toward the others for a couple of seconds and waved its tentacles in the air as if to say "I found them!" Less than a minute later, all six of the monsters were clustered around the shoreline facing the water.

We could take them all right now, Cris thought. He glanced toward Maura, caught her attention, and saw her make a sweeping motion with her right arm in firing position, indicating she was thinking the same thing. But both of them knew better than to attack. What they were about to gain could be much more important than the deaths of a half-dozen xenoborgs.

The two largest creatures — both of which had grenade launchers visible jutting out of "portholes" in their flanks — moved back from the shoreline about fifteen feet, which had the benefit of allowing Cris and Maura an unobstructed view of what the other four were doing.

Two of the monsters remaining by the stream dropped their tentacles in the stream and began wiggling them to agitate the water slightly. Then the other two, the pair with the longest extremities, began to reach out and pluck the silver things from the surface of the stream one by one.

In a matter of seconds, each of the pair of "catchers" had three of the things in its grasp. The two creatures pivoted, almost in unison, and shuffled the short distance back to where the two largest creatures were sitting . . . waiting. Cris and Maura could clearly see what the catcher closer to them was doing.

With a free tentacle, it pulled back a fold of flesh on the larger creature's body just behind the snout. Then it gently but firmly shoved the three silver things into the cavity that had been uncovered. Judging by the similarity of movements, Cris assumed the other catcher was doing the same thing to — for? — the other large xenoborg.

The catchers made one more trip to the shoreline, snapped up the remaining half-dozen silver objects, and repeated the insertion process on the other side of the big monsters' bodies. All the while, the six of them seemed oblivious to the possibility that they might be in danger or under observation.

Was whatever they were doing so important that they didn't bother to keep a watch over the area, or were they remaining alert even though they didn't seem to be cognizant of what might be going on around them?

Cris wished there was a way to answer that question without attracting the xenoborgs' attention himself, but he wasn't about to conduct research at the cost of his and Maura's safety. They had the information they had hoped for — or at least as much as they were going to get — and all that remained for them to do was wait for the xeno-borgs to move out of the area and then get back to the base as fast as they could.

Their business apparently completed, the monsters shuffled away, still following the stream, with the carriers in the lead, the two grenade-toting creatures in the middle, and the two long-tentacled ones bringing up the rear.

They once again appeared to be aware, even vigilant, elevating their extremities and waving them as they moved in the on-the-lookout posture that was characteristic of the way the creatures conducted themselves. Despite the fact that he and Maura had never been in any real danger, a flood of relief washed over Cris as the trailing monster vanished from sight.

"What do you think?" he asked Maura as they both left their hiding places and started to head northeast again.

Her first response was a giggle that she could only partially suppress. "I think I'm in love with the world's first cybernetic pincushion," she said, and then laughed again.

Cris looked down at his body and couldn't keep from laughing himself. Sticking out of the thin, soft outer layer of his artificial skin were dozens of thorns and thistles he had picked up while moving into and out of his hiding place.

"Do I look as dumb as I feel?" he asked.

"Judging by your tone of voice, I don't think that

would be possible, dear." Maura pulled one of the thistles from his upper arm and giggled again. "Let's go. You walk and I'll pluck."

"Don't tell anybody about this, okay?"

"Aw . . . not even Tony?"

"*Especially* not Tony!"

8

March 18, 2037

So easy . . . too easy, perhaps?

No. The Master dismissed that thought as quickly as it occurred. Almost since the day when Its xenoborgs had descended on this planet, nothing about this conquest had been easy.

The vile alien inched Its way along the rocky terrain that dominated the world It currently called home, Its body oscillating in a peculiar fashion due to the random movement of Its many tentacles. The creature was hungry, and It was not interested in obtaining nourishment in the usual way. There was a craving to satisfy, and It would not rest until that had been achieved.

The ground sloped downward, causing the wormlike creature to pause momentarily. Then, with no further hesitation, It proceeded on in the same fashion, in the same direction, only within seconds It was undulating in a body of clear, yellow-tinged liquid. It moved slowly, one of Its few limitations, and certainly an annoying one when there was an appetite to curb. Ah, well, It could always use the time to dwell on the current state of affairs. . . .

The newest plan It had developed would finally put an end to the resistance of these humans. Even if some of them survived the offensive, they would find themselves with nothing left to live for. And they too would soon die and decay, suffering deaths more prolonged and more horrible than if they had been exterminated by the Master's minions in the first place. That thought almost brought the loathsome creature to an abrupt halt, so caught up was It in Its enjoyment of the prospect of watching these impudent Earth-dwellers suffer exquisite, lingering torture before finally succumbing right before Its eyes. All three of the suckerlike mouths of the slithering mass of evil began to salivate at once. One of the few things It had always found hard to control was Its almost erotic enjoyment of the mere thought of watching another life form — almost any would do — squirm and scream with intense pain. And when they begged and pleaded and groveled — oh, the pleasure they gave It was almost too intense to withstand.

After a short time the Master began to move again, deciding to save Its fantasizing for later when, if all went right, it would serve as foreplay for the final scene — one It hoped to draw out for just the right amount of time.

In time, the planet would recover. But when the world was again fertile and lush and ready to be used, no trace of humankind would remain. The planet would belong to the Master, as it was always meant to be.

The Master had always known that It could make the xenoborgs do anything It wanted them to. Nevertheless, it was reassured by the success of the recent trials that had been conducted. Yes, xenoborgs could be made to attack stupidly and blindly, without regard for their survival or safety. Yes, they could be "persuaded" to crush and trample anything in their path, regardless of whether they were hungry or whether the things they were destroying had any food value or strategic importance. Both of these behaviors went against the orders that the Master had originally given to Its troops, but the troops didn't care. They would do what they were instructed to do, even if it killed them.

It allowed Itself a moment of self-satisfied pleasure as It contemplated the way in which xenoborgs and humans were similar. Both species had a much higher opinion of themselves than they deserved to hold. Both thought themselves capable of independent thought and decision-making. Neither group was consciously aware of the Master's existence, of the role that It was playing in the conquest of this world. But soon both of them would experience the full scope and power of the Master's capabilities, and when that experience was over the Master would reign supreme.

A few more details and a bit more preparation were in store before the plan to devastate the planet these humans seemed to love so dearly could be implemented. First, the xenoborgs had to be massed into large groups so that the Master could exert Its control over thousands of them at once, instead of contacting each small enclave one by one. That part of the preparation was already under way. (It almost chuckled at the thought of what Earth's mutated soldiers would think when they saw an impenetrable wall of creatures moving across their land, destroying everything in sight. What was the expression humans used at times like that — "holy shit"? For all of Its extraordinary intellectual powers, the creature was unable to comprehend how those two words came to be combined into an expression of awe.)

Second, because the number of xenoborgs on the planet was not sufficient to bring about the worldwide destruction the Master intended, It had to augment Its troops. Because the humans had firgured out a way to destroy the transport vessels It had used earlier in the offensive, the Master would find it inconvenient — although certainly not impossible — to send down more vessels containing more xenoborgs. And, in any event, for the purpose It intended to achieve, that step was not necessary. It had all the troops It could ever need already waiting on the surface of the planet, and it would be easy to take advantage of their availability.

It had reached Its destination. The Master was looking forward to spending the next several weeks in a new home, of sorts. The screaming began as soon as they realized It was in the area. Poor, miserable creatures, It thought. If they had any brains, they would be honored to serve as Its hosts. Ah well. . . .

The creature usually spent some time selecting which organism It would grace with its occupation, but there was no patience for that sort of thing today. After making a quick choice and telepathically indicating to the caretakers which of the caged beings It wished to occupy, the Master entered the cave and rested beside the throne to await the preparations.

As It waited, It continued to dwell on Its impending victory. If the soon-to-be-extinct inhabitants of Earth hadn't given up by then, the sheer sight of Its new troops would be almost enough to make them submit to the inevitable. And if the humans had half the collective brain power they seemed to exhibit, they would do just that.

After a time the caretakers entered the cave, their prisoner struggling frantically against the vinelike bonds that covered most of the being's asymmetrical body. The now-screaming prisoner was deposited on the throne and then securely bound to it. All that was allowed to remain free was the large, contorted mouth, through which the Master's involuntary host alternately screamed and cried and pleaded.

The Master always loved these little displays of terror. Such was Its nature. But today It was ravenous, and there was other, greater terror soon to be enjoyed. Without wasting much time, the Master set about the task of boring Its way into the prisoner's body where It would stay for as long as it took Its three mouths to extract every ounce of body fluid therein.

To the absolute despair of Its unwilling host, the process would take a few weeks, if measured in Earth time. Enough time for It to finalize the plans for destroying the planet. Plans that would make the whole process an easy one.

Almost too easy. . . .

9

March 19, 2037

Tony strode into the briefing room and headed straight for where Cris was standing, holding his right fist in the air and shaking it in a menacing fashion.

"If you *ever* stay out late again and worry me like that—"

"We were having so much fun, we just lost track of the time," Cris said with affected innocence. He wasn't sure from Tony's posture and his tone of voice whether his friend was serious or not, but he tried to play the situation for a joke and see what happened.

Tony unclenched his fist and lowered his hand as he came to a stop in front of Cris. His shoulders seemed to slump, as though he was trying to release the tension that had been building up in him.

When he spoke again, Cris knew his earlier remark had been more serious than jesting.

"We *were* worried, Cris. I knew you could take care of yourself, but still, you were gone for a lot longer than we thought you'd be. Nobody's invincible, you know."

"I know, Tony. And I'm sorry, really. But we did lose track of time, sort of. We kept waiting, hoping something interesting would happen. I think you would have done the same thing," Cris said inoffensively.

"And if I had," Tony shot back, "and you were the one back here waiting, you'd be just as upset as I am right now."

"You're right," Cris said, sincerely contrite. "But try to calm down, okay? All's well that ends well."

That sounded like something John would have said, Tony thought. He was about to voice that impression when he remembered that Richard was in the room. Instead he said, "And you're right, too. I'm glad you're okay, pal. That's all that matters."

"Good to see you again . . . Cris." Richard, sensing that the conversation between his superiors was over, stepped up beside Tony and delivered his own welcome in a purposely casual tone. He was in the process of raising his right hand to his forehead in a salute when he got to the word "again." Then he paused, lowered his hand to waist height, and held it out as he spoke Cris's name.

"You too, Richard. Thanks." Cris shook the corporal's hand, more than a little mystified by what had just happened — perplexed but pleased at the same time.

At that point Maura walked into the room. "Well, now the gang's all here," said Tony, turning to greet her. "Why so late, dear? Couldn't decide what to wear?"

"Oh, cut it out," Maura said with feigned exasperation. "If you must know," she said proudly, "I've been taking some special tests."

"Tests, huh?" Tony asked suspiciously. "Just what did you two do while you were all alone in the wilderness?"

"Wouldn't you like to know?" said Cris, stepping forward and taking Maura's hand.

"Yeah, I would. Tell me, or I'll make something up!"

The conversation came to an abrupt halt as Traynor walked into the briefing room followed by General Ernest Garrison, the commander of the Manitowoc base. Richard immediately turned toward the two men and stiffened into a posture of attention. The other three cyborgs looked over to acknowledge the general's presence but then began moving toward nearby chairs, anticipating what the man was about to say.

"At ease, corporal," the general muttered in an offhand manner. "Be seated, all of you." General Garrison was a military man through and through, but he had long since learned — more precisely, become resigned to — the fact that most of the cybernetic soldiers in his command did not share that outlook. He had accepted that how they conducted themselves in the field was more important than whether or not they called him "sir" and threw him a salute. He had changed to the point where he often didn't mind dispensing with protocol and procedure. Military jargon could be cumbersome at best and misleading at worst, and one thing he didn't want these soldiers to do was misunderstand anything he had to say to them.

The general and Traynor took seats facing the four cyborgs. Garrison glanced down at a sheaf of papers in his lap, cleared his throat, and spoke.

"I have some things to tell you. After that, you can speak freely, ask questions, unless you're instructed to do otherwise. By the time we leave this room, I want to have enough information to devise a plan for how to get rid of these powwers."

"Powers?" Cris and Tony blurted out the one-word question simultaneously, automatically.

The general scowled — he had barely begun, and already he was being interrupted! Traynor, appreciating Cris and Tony's puzzlement because they were unfamiliar with this use of the word, spoke up before Garrison could react verbally.

"The silver things," he explained. When the general didn't break in, he continued. "We're calling them 'powwers' — spelled with two W's, in case you ever have to write the word. They definitely have something to do with power, of the electrical sort, and we're starting to realize that these things may be an even greater enemy to us than the xenoborgs themselves."

The general harrumphed again, irritated now because Traynor was getting into the territory his own presentation was supposed to cover. Traynor sat back and let the commander continue.

"Here's what we know," he began, "or what we think we can logically deduce.

"Powwers are definitely not native to this planet, probably organic but not intelligent. They have the ability to ingest and store electromagnetic radiation, and to release it at a later time in the form of electrical energy.

"They have a biological relationship with xenoborgs that appears to be symbiotic rather than parasitic. That is, each life form relies on the other.

"Xenoborgs use the electrical energy that powwers accumulate, and when a powwer's energy becomes depleted, the xenoborg sees to it that the thing is recharged. So the powwer continues to survive, thanks to the xenoborg, and the xenoborg continues to be able to make use of the energy the powwer can contain.

"Whether they're in use or simply being stored for transport, powwers are carried in concealed cavities inside the xenoborgs' bodies. Because xenoborg flesh is a poor conductor of electricity, it's impossible to tell by visual or electronic sensing means whether a certain xenoborg is carrying or using powwers, or how fully charged the powwers inside it might be.

"Any xenoborg can transport powwers, but not every xenoborg uses them. The organic functions of xenoborgs are biochemical in nature, just like those of human beings; the creatures do not need infusions of electricity in order to survive."

The general paused and leaned forward in his chair, a characteristic trait that indicated his next statement would be a blockbuster. Cris and Maura weren't surprised when they heard it, though, because they already had a good idea what General Garrison was leading up to.

"The xenoborgs that *do* use powwers are the leader-types — the ones that carry weaponry and sensory equipment. All of their devices do require electricity. Although they have inorganic batteries that can store and release some electrical energy, the batteries are probably only used as a reserve. The energy that keeps a xenoborg's technology in working order comes from powwers. As long as they are continuously resupplied with freshly charged powwers, these creatures can operate their weapons and gadgets indefinitely. If they are deprived of this energy source, they become ordinary xenoborgs."

General Garrison paused again, this time signaling that he had reached the end of his monologue. Traynor took the cue. "Opinions and questions, people."

Tony burst in with a question that had been on his mind for quite a while. "How come the xenoborgs can handle them without getting shocked? When Cris tried to pick one up—"

"That's just part of the symbiotic relationship," Traynor said. "Apparently the powwers have some unconscious, innate way of sensing when they're being touched by a xenoborg. If any other solid object comes into contact with them, they react within a fraction of a second, bleeding off enough of their charge to discourage the intruder."

"That's putting it mildly," Cris interjected. "The jolt I took would probably have electrocuted a human being."

"We know, Cris," said Traynor. "Some people have found that out the hard way."

"What happens when their charge is depleted?" asked Maura.

"We don't know from experience," said Traynor. "We've never heard of anyone encountering a powwer that didn't have at least a trickle of electricity left in it. If the charged state is their normal condition — and we assume it is — then it stands to reason that if one runs out of power, it dies."

"How do they get recharged?" Richard asked.

"Sunlight," Cris blurted before Traynor had a chance to answer. "Solar power."

"This is something we don't fully understand,"

Traynor continued. "but by piecing together various bits of information — including what Cris and Maura found out yesterday — we have an answer that sounds good. When a powwer needs a new dose of energy, it is extracted from the xenoborg's body and deposited in a liquid medium, usually water, in a place where it can soak up illumination from the sun. Recharging takes anywhere from a few hours to a full day, depending on the intensity of the sunlight that hits the surface of the thing's body."

"Solar power I understand," said Tony. "But why water?"

"Again, we're not sure," Traynor answered. "Our best guess is that a liquid medium is desirable because when powwers recharge, they flatten their bodies to present as much area to the sunlight as possible, and it's easier to perform this shape-changing while floating in liquid than it would be to flatten themselves out if they were lying on solid ground. Of course, water is also a very good conductor, so they might be able to accelerate the recharging process by pulling in energy from the liquid around them in addition to getting it through the air. Whatever the reason, it does seem apparent that both a source of sunlight and a source of water must be available for them to replace their used-up energy."

"I'm trying to understand exactly what we saw," said Cris. "Tell me if I've got this right: Two nights ago, we saw a xenoborg come to a recharging spot and pick up about half of the powwers that were floating in the stream. The monster left the others behind because—"

"Because they weren't charged up all the way yet," Tony interrupted.

"That's probably right," said Traynor, directing his response to Cris after raising an eyebrow in Tony's direction.

Cris went on. "And after they got a few more hours of sun the next morning, the others were also fully charged, so when the group of xenoborgs came by they scooped them up."

Traynor nodded. "And if you had stayed there for a few more hours — although I'm not suggesting you should have — you might have seen another xenoborg, or a group of them, stop by to drop off a new bunch of powwers for recharging. From what you reported, that spot in the stream seems like a prime location for this sort of activity. The water is calm, so the powwers will stay where they're put. The area gets strong sunlight, on a clear day, from shortly after sunrise until some time fairly late in the afternoon."

"So why don't we just stake the place out and blow them to bits when they get dumped off?" Tony asked

The general answered that question; this wasn't the first time he had seen fit to chastise Sergeant S-24 for his impetuosity, and it probably wouldn't be the last. "Because, sergeant, we don't want them to know how much we know. If we made them aware that we had discovered one of their recharging spots, they'd simply abandon it and find another one. It wouldn't do us a damn bit of good to destroy a couple dozen of these things when there are thousands and thousands of them in use." General Garrison's voice was dripping with condescension as he finished, and Tony was thoroughly humbled, at least for the moment.

"What we need," Cris said slowly, thoughtfully, "is a way to strike simultaneously at as many recharging spots, or probable recharging spots, as possible."

"A correct, if obvious, deduction," said Traynor. "But how do we accomplish that? There are roughly a thousand Cyborg Commandos operating in this little part of the world. The most conservative estimate is that we're outnumbered twenty to one by xenoborgs, and anywhere from ten to twenty-five percent of those are equipped with lasers, grenade launchers, pulser rifles, sensors and communication devices all designed to reduce a CC to his or her component parts. How do we cover every body of standing water in the midwestern United States — and even if we could, how would we occupy all of those objectives until every powwer ran out of —power?"

No one spoke for several seconds. It was obvious from the way Traynor asked his question that he wasn't playing games with the four CCs in the room. Neither he nor the general had an answer. Identifying the task was easy; figuring out how to perform it was something else altogether.

Then, from a most unexpected source, came two words that changed the course of history.

"The people," said Richard Adams, almost too low for Traynor and Garrison to hear.

"What?" asked Traynor instinctively.

"Speak up, son!" said the general gruffly, intimidating the corporal without meaning to.

"The people," Richard repeated, louder but more hesitant than before. "Has anybody thought about using the people?"

"Yeahhh!" said Tony, drawing out the word. "We may be outnumbered, but they're not!"

"But they're defenseless," said General Garrison.

Cris's mind raced back to the first night of the invasion, to the vision of his stepmother standing at a window, screaming and jabbing at a monster with a ski pole. Minutes later she was dead — but she had not died passively. She had not given up without a fight. . . .

"No, general," Cris said quietly. "You're not defenseless until you're dead."

10

March 19, 2037

The briefing broke up about an hour after Richard had suggested using humans to help fight the aliens. By that time, the six participants had made some progress toward devising a plan to render the silver things useless.

While Traynor and General Garrison headed off, presumably to discuss the idea further with military strategists, the four CCs were left to do what they wanted for a few hours before receiving orders for their next excursion into the field. It was a good opportunity for them to have their own informal briefing, getting each other caught up on their recent experiences. But, naturally, the first topic of conversation between them was the plan they had just helped to formulate.

"On one level, it makes a lot of sense," said Cris when Tony prompted him for an opinion. "Like you pointed out just after Richard had his idea, we do outnumber the xenoborgs if you count in the human population. The key is figuring out the best way to make that fact work to our advantage."

"And our idea of the 'best way' has to be something that most people will agree with," Maura pointed out. "Whether the plan makes sense to us or not doesn't really matter. Whatever the experts eventually decide to do, we'll need thousands of people working to pull it off, just in this little section of the world. If we can't find that many people who are willing to risk their lives, then we're beaten before we start."

"Maybe I should have kept quiet," said Richard glumly. After making his remark about using human civilians, he had participated very little in the ensuing conversation. As with most planning discussions, the talk had centered around methods that wouldn't work. It was a process of elimination, examining and discarding unworkable alternatives in the hope of eventually arriving at a plan that would succeed.

And as the conversation continued, Richard found himself hoping that the process of elimination would eliminate everything. Instead of being encouraged by the fact that his idea was being used as the nucleus of the discussion, he was torn by anxiety and regret. Practically every application of his idea that someone suggested had been shot down by someone else. But sooner or later, he said to himself, they'd figure out something. And then . . . he didn't want to think about the consequences.

"No — I'm glad you said something," said Tony firmly. "I can't believe we didn't think of this earlier. We haven't been using all of our living resources because we were convinced that humans wouldn't stand a chance against the aliens. We didn't even stop to consider that there may be ways to use what's left of the world population without putting it in danger of becoming extinct."

"But we all spent an hour coming up with lots of plans that wouldn't work. It was a waste of time — pointless discussion based on a bad idea," Richard said, trying to convince himself as well as the others with his words.

"But we did hit on a couple of plans that seemed promising," Cris said. "Why don't you take your own advice, Richard? Leave the heavy brain work up to the experts. You gave them something to think about — now let them do the second-guessing." Richard could tell that his teammates had not figured out the real reason for his distress — which was understandable, since he hadn't put it into words for them.

The corporal was silent for a moment. Then he spoke softly and slowly, as though what he said was being pulled from deep within himself. "I've never been an idea person," he said. "I've always been better at following orders than figuring out what the orders should be. That's why I enlisted in the first place. The military is a good place for someone like me — I do what I'm told, and someone else takes the responsibility."

"I think that may be what's bothering you," Maura said gently.

Richard knew right away what she was talking about, and he confirmed her suspicions. "If any kind of plan comes out of my idea, thousands of people are going to die — and maybe a lot of us, too. I can't go through the rest of my life knowing that my one stupid remark was the cause of all that. I should have kept my mouth shut," he said again, becoming very agitated.

"Aw, don't give yourself so much credit," said Tony, hitting on a way to lighten the situation. "Look at it this way: If you hadn't thought of using the people, it would have occurred to someone else sooner or later. Why don't you just pretend it wasn't your idea? When the orders come down, we'll all follow them as well as we can, and it won't matter why they were given or where they came from."

"I've never been good at pretending," Richard said.

"I'm not talking about looking at the world through rose-colored sensors," Tony countered. "But you gotta stop worrying about things you can't do anything about. You said the words, you can't take them back, and you shouldn't want to. The Cyborg Commando Force is the best thing that ever happened to the human race, considering what's taken place in the last couple of years. But we can't solve the world's problems by ourselves; if we could, the xenoborgs would be dead and gone by now. We need help — and we have to hope that we can get it, somehow, from all the men and women out there who are still alive and have a desire to keep on living. If I was the one who came up with your idea, I'd be proud of it."

Cris had never heard Tony sound more serious and more sincere, and he was deeply affected by his friend's words.

"I just can't stand the thought of those slimy bastards slaughtering any more helpless people. Ever since . . ." His voice dropped to a whisper, and Richard stopped short. He had obviously not intended to say as much as he had.

"It's too late, Richard," said Maura. "You started to tell us something, and I have a feeling there's a lot more to it."

"And when she has a feeling," Cris cut in without thinking, "you better believe it."

"Huh?" asked Richard.

"I'm sorry, Maura," said Cris, remembering how she hated discussing her "feelings" in front of other people.

"Don't be," she told him. "It's time I started facing up to what's inside me instead of doubting it or wishing it wasn't there."

Cris was surprised. "I'm glad to hear you say that, but what brought it on?"

"Well, it has to do with the tests I took."

"Would someone mind letting the rest of us in on what's going on?" Tony asked.

When Maura didn't respond to that right away, Cris hesitantly said, "In the morning when we were by the stream—"

"Let me tell it, Cris." Maura turned to Tony and continued, forgetting Richard's unfinished thought for the moment. "Remember when we were on the 'Chase Into Space' mission, when I got that feeling about . . . about what had happened to John?"

"Yeah," said Tony solemnly. "I know what you're talking about. I couldn't buy it at the time, but—"

"Neither could I, not completely. That's the point. I've been getting these feelings — that's the only way I can describe them — for a long time. Sometimes an image forms in my mind, and I can 'see' something without using my eyes. Most of the time it's not that substantial — just a glimmer of a thought, an inkling that something . . . different . . . is happening or about to happen.

"I never gave it much consideration while I was growing up. I figured it was something like woman's intuition, and that a lot of people had these 'feelings' once in a while. When my feelings turned out to be right, I chalked it up to dumb luck or coincidence. When they turned out to be wrong — which was most of the time — it added to my impression that there was nothing to them in the first place. Once in a while I made the mistake of confiding in someone about a feeling I had, and almost every time I did that I ended up embarrassed or hurt when things didn't work out the way I predicted they were going to. . . ."

Maura paused as a flood of painful memories came back. Cris, interpreting the silence correctly, jumped in with a remark that he hoped would encourage her. "Sometimes things do work out," he said. "You should have more faith in yourself."

"That's basically what the people in the psychogenic testing center told me," she responded, forcing her mind back to the present. "I get premonitions just like everyone else, and most of the time they turn out to be meaningless or just plain wrong. But beyond that, I have some kind of ability to know when something special is going to happen."

"So you took some tests, and you passed?" asked Tony.

"They're not the kind of tests you pass or fail. It's not that straightforward. The thing is, everybody's got the potential for psychogenic ability; it's something that we all have in common as part of the way we think. But some people are more sensitive to it than others. Some people can recognize it when it happens to them, and the ones who are really good at it can identify their vague feelings and then refine them into specific thoughts and images."

"And you're one of those people," Cris said.

"No. Not yet, anyway. I have the sensitivity, but I haven't learned how to distinguish between the two types of 'feelings' — the ones that are just manifestations of my fears and expectations, and the ones that really come from within."

"What about the stream?" asked Tony abruptly, recalling what Cris had mentioned at the start of this part of the conversation.

"That was a good example," she said. "Something inside me told me that we shouldn't leave at sunrise, like we had planned to do. While I was sitting in the dark, staring at the silver things in the water, I got the impression that they weren't just going to stay floating there indefinitely — something was going to happen. But I didn't know what, and I didn't know when. All I knew was that I was very uncomfortable with the idea of heading back to this base when the sun came up."

"So you talked Cris into staying," said Tony.

"I didn't *have* to talk him into it," she said, slightly irritated.

"What happened was that she had the courage to tell me about her feeling," said Cris. "And something inside *me* said that maybe we should stick around and see if something did happen."

"Does that mean you're psychogenic, too?" Tony asked.

"No, it means that I respected her feelings, even though I didn't share them with her," Cris said.

"That's right," Maura said approvingly. "If you had ignored or disregarded what was going on inside me and insisted that we leave, I would have gone along with the decision without an argument — because I wouldn't have had enough faith in myself to protest. Your vote of confidence was what got me over the hump. When I got back here and made my report, I included all the information about the feeling I had, and I asked to talk to someone who could help me figure out what was going on inside my head. They set up an appointment for me in the psychogenic testing center, and you pretty much know the rest of the story from there."

"So we have a mind-reader in our midst, eh?" cracked Tony.

"No — and thank God I can't read yours," Maura said tauntingly. Then she went on, serious again. "I can't read anyone else's thoughts. I can't predict the future. I can't move an object from one place to another without touching it. All I can do — and it doesn't seem like much — is occasionally get a sense of when something out of the ordinary has happened or is going to happen. What I have to do now is try to stay in touch with my thoughts and impressions, try to be very sensitive to everything, and figure out a way to sort out the psychogenic feelings from the emotional ones."

"Don't take this the wrong way," Tony said. "But does this mean that when you get a feeling, we have to go along with it?"

"Not at all. The pressure's not on you, it's on me. I promise I won't mention anything about a feeling unless I'm at least fairly sure it means something. And anything we do as a team is still going to be a group decision, just like it's always been."

"Fair enough," Tony said agreeably. "But do me a favor, okay? If you ever get a feeling, even the slightest little indication, that some young, unattached female cyborg is looking for a mechanical companion, would you be so kind as to point me in her direction?"

Cris laughed. "I wondered how long it would take you to figure out a way to benefit from this."

"About that long, pal. Hey, Maura, here's a thought. When all this is over, how about you and me setting up a matchmaking service?"

"That might be a real good idea, Tony."

"Oh, yeah?" He was taken off guard by her serious response to his facetious question.

"Yeah. If I can find a match for you, I can find a match for anybody."

* * *

The conversation took a more serious turn after that as Cris related the story of the rampaging xenoborgs he and Maura had witnessed during their night in the wilderness — how they trampled and tore up everything in their way. Tony and Richard listened without interrupting, but when Cris's monologue was over the questions came fast and furious.

"How come we haven't heard about this before now?" Tony asked.

"As far as I know, this is the first time something like this has happened, or at least the first time any of us have ever seen such a thing," said Cris. "I've scanned all the recent updates on the computer network, and no other CC base has reported anything similar to what we saw."

"What do the experts have to say about it?" asked Richard.

"I don't think they're taking it lightly," answered Maura. "But I don't get the impression they're terribly worried about it, either. I guess I can't blame them, since they don't have a lot to go on."

"Unless we find out it has happened more than once," Cris added, "there's no reason to suspect that it was anything more than an isolated, random incident. Anyway, that's what they told us, pretty much word for word, after we reported it." His voice was liberally tinged with disgust, and Tony picked up on that mood.

"But you don't go along with that, do you?"

"I don't know what to think. I understand their point of view — but they didn't *see* it. They have our computer tapes and our verbal reports, but I don't think they have a real good idea of how horrible it was to watch those monsters do what they did."

"Why didn't you stop them?" Richard said.

"We could have, maybe," said Maura. "But first of all, we were there to keep the silver things — the powwers — under surveillance, and if we gave ourselves away we wouldn't have been able to accomplish that objective. Second of all, speaking for myself at least, I was kind of in shock when I saw what they were doing. They were destroying everything in front of them. . . . I just kept wishing they would stop."

"But they did stop," said Tony.

"Yeah," said Cris. "I'm glad they did, but I can't figure out why. Nothing intercepted them or challenged them. They could have kept on trampling and tearing all the way to Lake Michigan if they wanted to."

"Maybe that's the key," Richard suggested. "They did it because they *wanted* to. They had their fun, they got bored, and they stopped."

"It could be that simple," said Maura. "For the sake of the world, I hope so. If every xenoborg on Earth got it in its head to just start ripping and tearing and smashing things, I can't imagine what would happen."

"Unfortunately," said Tony, "I think I can. And it scares the hell out of me."

11

March 24, 2037

"I've had mixed emotions before," said Tony as he sank to a sitting position, "but they're more than mixed right now — they're downright scrambled."

In the course of four different search-and-destroy missions in the last several days in and around Manitowoc, Tony and his comrades had done a whole lot of searching but absolutely no destroying. Most of the other CC teams operating out of the Manitowoc base had experienced a similar lack of results in the same period of time. Xenoborgs were becoming harder and harder to locate, not only around the city but apparently throughout the entire upper Midwest.

"They seem to be gone, but they can't be," Maura observed. "Twenty thousand monsters don't just disappear."

"As much as we wish they would!" Tony responded. "I'd be happy if I never laid eyes on one of them again — but I know they're still out here somewhere, and I want to find them before they find me."

"Look on the bright side," said Richard. "The less time we spend tracking xenoborgs, the more time we have to spend carrying out our standing orders. Every person we recruit brings us a little closer to being able to put the plan into motion."

Richard Adams had changed his attitude considerably in the last week. Unbeknownst to him, Tony had talked to Cris and Maura about Richard's feelings of hostility from the other members of his team.

"We really haven't accepted him. But what does he expect?" Cris asked during one of the three friends' conversations.

"I think he expects us to respect him for his own good qualities and to quit comparing him to John," Maura said gently.

"There's no comparison," Cris snapped, and was immediately sorry for it. "I didn't mean to take it out on you," he told Maura, taking her hand and squeezing it gently.

"I know," she responded warmly. "But we have to quit taking our grief for John out on Richard," she said firmly.

"I have a feeling that man is carrying around some heavy grief of his own," Tony said solemnly.

"Hey, I'm the one who's supposed to have the 'feelings,' remember?" Maura teased.

"Yeah, well this one has nothing to do with your psychic abilities, hotshot," Tony countered. "Richard let his guard down a little when the two of us were talking while you were out watching xenoborgs tearing up the countryside."

"What did he say?" Cris asked.

"It's not what he said so much as what he *didn't* say," Tony answered seriously.

"Damn!" Maura exclaimed suddenly. "He started to say something when we were talking after the briefing and I was going to try to draw him out, but then we all got sidetracked. Remember?"

"Now that you mention it, yeah," Cris said sadly. "Another example of our habitual lack of regard for the man."

The three of them decided then and there that they would all try to treat their newest teammate like they treated each other. As soon as they started acting that way, the gesture did not go unnoticed by Richard, who seemed to be relaxing around them more and more all the time.

It didn't hurt a bit that General Garrison had congratulated Richard personally, in front of hundreds of his peers, for coming up with the idea of recruiting civilian humans to help fight the aliens. From that seed had sprung a full-blown plan that seemed to have a decent chance of succeeding. Once the strategists in the Cyborg Commando

Force began to consider the resource they had all overlooked — the rest of the human race — it didn't take long at all for them to devise a way to use that resource.

There were still obstacles to be surmounted, of course. For the plan to work, tons of material supplies had to be gathered, including a whole lot of rubber and plastic, neither of which were as readily available as other substances such as stone, metal, and wood. And thousands of people had to be recruited — approached, convinced that they should cooperate, and then counted on keep their promises and show up in the required places at the required times. The plan was vulnerable to failure for a dozen different reasons — but, as the military experts had told all the CCs in their briefings on the subject, this was a typical trait of any large-scale operation. Even with its shortcomings and potential drawbacks, "Operation Manpower" represented the best chance mankind had for first neutralizing the powwers and then wiping out the xenoborgs.

As part of the preparation for implementing the plan, every team of CCs was given two standing orders — instructions that would remain in effect until expressly cancelled by counter-orders. When they weren't otherwise engaged while on field excursions, they were supposed to be searching for caches of usable materials and seeking out any people they might be able to recruit.

One of the drawbacks to the plan was that it had to be conveyed to the population by word of mouth, certainly an inefficient and time-consuming way of spreading information and enlisting volunteers. But in the absence of mass media — radio, television, and newspapers had been virtually nonexistent since the invasion — this was the only way to achieve the goal. And, according to the experts, this was probably just as well; if news of the plan were broadcast or disseminated to the public at large in writing, it wouldn't take long for the xenoborgs to intercept the information, and that would doom the effort to failure before it could really begin.

As Richard had listened to the strategists explain all the details of the plan they had devised, all the intricacies, all the safeguards they had built in to reduce the risk of failure and death, he was impressed and almost amazed by how thorough the experts had been. They had taken his two words — "The people" — and used them as the foundation for a body of theory, the framework of a structure that, when it was built, would come crashing down on the invaders with the combined power of the Cyborg Commando Force *and* the rest of the human race.

Just as Tony had urged him to do, Richard had stopped feeling self-conscious about his idea and had become quite proud of the contribution he had made. He didn't strut around crowing about it — he hadn't changed *that* much — but he had stopped worrying about his responsibility and the chance of failure. It was a good plan, thanks to what the experts had done with his idea, and it would work. That was not only the correct frame of mind, Richard told himself, it was the only possible outlook. If the plan didn't succeed, no one would hold Richard Adams responsible for having started the whole thing . . . because all too soon there would be no one left.

* * *

When the recruiting effort started, Cris thought it resembled nothing so much as the stories he had read about the underground resistance in Europe during Earth's last world war almost a century ago. The citizens of the occupied countries couldn't stand up and fight their oppressors directly, or they would have been blown to bits. Instead, they gathered furtively, in small groups, and plotted and carried out acts of subterfuge that were at least irritating and at best debilitating to the enemy.

What the resistance fighters accomplished did not impress Cris as much as the idea of the resistance itself. He could relate in a personal way, because shortly after the alien invasion he and Tony had joined a group of self-proclaimed "bug swatters" who intended to take to the hills with a small collection of firearms and then engage in hit-and-run assaults against any groups of monsters they came across.

The idea was an honorable one. The members of that group had their hearts in the right place. But they found out, quickly and tragically, that a group of men with rifles and pistols stood virtually no chance against even two or three xenoborgs. Small-caliber bullets had no effect on the monsters, apparently because they had no such thing as vital organs. The leader of the group, who was fanatical in his determination, stood and pumped round after round into an approaching monster — right up until the moment when the creature engulfed and crushed him.

Cris and Tony, along with the rest of the group, turned and fled when they realized how fruitless it was to try to fight the invaders with conventional hand weapons. That was the end of their brief careers as resistance fighters — until now. Now, thanks to the technology that could produce Cyborg Commandos, they were much better equipped not only to take part in, but to be in the forefront of, a counteroffensive.

This plan of resistance, like the first one Cris had been involved with, required the participation of human beings who were willing to risk their lives so that others might survive. But this time the weapons of the resistance were much more subtle. The plan did not call for human beings to kill anything directly, but rather indirectly. Instead of guns, knives, and explosives, they would use sheets, tarpaulins, and nets. . . .

But before things got to that stage, the CCs had to round up people. *Lots* of people — at least fifty thousand able-bodied men and women, the experts figured, just to put the plan into effect in this small section of North America, and at least that many more in each of the dozens of other areas around the world where the xenoborgs were most heavily concentrated.

Calculations indicated that each of the Cyborg Commandos attached to the Manitowoc base had to approach and persuade "only" twenty or thirty people, since regular soldiers would also be able to do a lot of that sort of work. And they had between three and five weeks to accomplish that. To the experts who had worked out the figures and the timing, it seemed like a job that could be done — and Cris had thought so too, at first. But now, a few days after the standing orders had been issued, he had begun to wonder if five weeks would be enough time. And the pessimistic part of him, which he found it impossible to keep submerged all the time, was starting to doubt if it could be done at all.

"We'd better not stay in one place too long," said Richard after the team had sat, mostly in silence, for about fifteen minutes. "People aren't going to walk up to us — we have to go to them."

Cris was beginning to appreciate Richard's contributions, even if the man did sometimes — all too often, in fact — state the obvious. Richard was energetic, determined, and hopeful, and he — the one who was supposed to be the leader of this team — was lucky to have a cyborg with Richard's qualities.

"He's right, gang. Time to get a move on," Cris said regretfully.

"Aw, a couple minutes more isn't going to make any difference," Tony said. "I was just getting into the scenery." Here, along the shore of Lake Michigan about two miles south of the outskirts of Manitowoc, the landscape and seascape were both devoid of any obvious evidence of the xenoborgs' presence on the planet. Since the initial onslaught, when monsters were liable to be encountered almost anywhere, the xenoborgs had pulled back for the most part and done most of their killing and wrecking around large metropolitan areas. The once-beautiful city of Milwaukee was one such area; it had been under alien occupation for more than two years, and the few people and CCs who had ventured in and come out again had nothing but horror stories to report about the carnage and destruction they had witnessed.

"Actually, Tony," Maura chided, "a couple of minutes might make a big difference. There might be a group of people moving through the woods a mile away from us right now. If we had started walking two minutes ago, we'd be where they are instead of sitting here where they aren't."

"Uh, oh," he said in return. "Do I feel a feeling coming on?"

"No. I just happen to agree with Richard."

"And so do I," Cris added, firming his resolve again. "Let's go." He stood and started walking south, making it clear that no further discussion was called for.

Tony quickened his pace, caught up with Cris, and fell into step beside him. "I really think we ought to change our approach," he said.

"What does that mean?"

"Well, we've got the dirty job here. Instead of being assigned to canvass small cities and villages like some of our illustrious comrades, we're supposed to dig up our fifty people apiece by combing the countryside — a countryside where we're the only intelligent life I've seen for the last three hours."

"So? What are you getting at?"

"People in the country are on the move, and we're traipsing around looking for them. Despite what Richard says, I think the best thing for us to do *is* stay in one place. We pick a spot close to a highway that seems like it might be fairly well traveled, and we wait for people to come by."

"It figures," said Maura. She and Richard had closed to within a couple of steps behind the pair and had overheard Tony's recommendation. "When you're lost and you want to be found, the best thing to do is stay put. When you move around, you make it that much harder for people to find you."

"But we're the ones doing the looking, not them," Richard said.

"The principle still applies," Cris said, punctuating the statement by coming to an abrupt stop and turning so that he could see all three of his teammates. "Let's find a road and pick a spot to use for our recruiting station."

"You're the boss," said Richard, and Cris immediately smiled to himself as he thought, You've come a long way, Corporal Adams. "But if this is the best way to find people, then why didn't they recommend it to us back at the base?"

"You just answered your own question," Cris said.

"Huh?"

"Back at the base," Cris continued. "That's the point. *They're* back at the base and *we're* out here. Those guys hear all our reports and review all our tapes, but some of them haven't been outside their sheltered environment since the bugs dropped from the sky.

"Despite all the information they have at their disposal, they don't really know, or at least they don't fully appreciate, what it's like outside. We *do* know what it's like, and sometimes we have to make decisions that only we are capable of making. Do you understand?"

"More and more all the time," said Richard warmly. "We gotta do what we gotta do. Right?"

"I couldn't have put it better myself," said Tony, resting a hand on the other man's shoulder. "You used to be a real good soldier, Richard."

"Used to be?"

"Yeah. Now you're getting to be a real good Cyborg Commando."

* * *

It took about an hour for the four cyborgs to find a suitable spot for their outpost: just inside a small grove of trees in a gentle valley about a hundred yards west of a two-lane road that ran north and south. The highway — probably a county road, although all the identifying signs had long since disappeared — was in reasonably good shape. The only signs of damage to the pavement were cracks and potholes that had almost certainly been caused by freezing and thawing over the last two winters. The driving surface had not been blasted into huge chunks or obstructed by fallen trees and boulders, as was the case along virtually all of the area's limited-access highways and main thoroughfares, where xenoborgs had done their best to paralyze transportation.

From where the CCs stationed themselves, they could see almost a half-mile of the roadway in either direction. With their auditory sensors turned up to extremely high sensitivity, they could hear the sound of an engine from at least a mile away, so they would have even more warning than their visual sensors could give them. Even a vehicle traveling at sixty miles per hour — an almost unheard-of speed in these times, when fuel conservation was paramount — could not cover the entire stretch of highway before one or more of the CCs could run the short distance to the roadside and try to flag it down.

"A good spot — with a nice view," said Tony, sitting down with his back against a tree and putting his hands behind his head.

"A good idea — I hope," said Cris.

And it turned out to be a good idea . . . even though the first living things they saw using the road were not human.

12

March 24, 2037

Thanks to their super-sensitive hearing, Cris, Maura, Tony, and Richard all knew the xenoborgs were coming about thirty seconds before the first monster crested the rise to the north and started to shuffle down the incline. By then, Cris had already devised and conveyed to the others a simple plan of action.

"Let them pass us," he whispered. "Let 'em go until they're out of sight again. Then we fan out, come up behind them, and—"

"We know the rest," Tony said.

Cris's plan was logical, and a more or less standard tactic for encounters with xenoborgs of unknown types. When you couldn't be sure which ones in a group had weapons — and it wasn't always easy to tell — the thing to do was get the drop on them from behind. The ones with weapons would have to pivot to get the attackers in view before they could bring their lasers or their grenades into use, and that small edge in time was all the CCs needed to cut the leaders to pieces.

Unfortunately, in this case Cris's orders were based on a bad assumption. He had expected the group to number no more than six or eight, the usual number of creatures in a xenoborg patrol. But by the time the lead creature in this bunch had reached the bottom of the valley, directly across from their hiding place, xenoborg number twenty-three was just coming over the crest of the hill. When he saw number ten, Cris had let out a muttered oath. Since then, all four of them had sat speechless and motionless as the parade passing before them took on more and more fearsome proportions.

It was Tony, characteristically, who broke the silence.

"What now, boss?" he whispered. "You still wanna sneak up behind them?"

"No. It's time for Plan B," Cris whispered back with mock seriousness.

"What's that?" asked Richard when Cris didn't immediately continue.

"Tony takes the first thirty, and we divide up the rest."

"Sounds like a sensible plan to me," Maura whispered.

"With all due respect, *sir*," Tony said, "I think I'd like to hear about Plan C."

"Okay," Cris said, all business again. "Here's an idea. Climb the tallest tree you can find and let me know if you can see the end of this caravan."

"I'm on my way," Tony said, already moving. There was a massive oak about twenty yards deeper into the grove that was at least eighty feet tall. If Tony could get close to the top of it, he would be able to see over the crest of the gradual slope to the north.

"Why do we need to know how many there are?" asked Maura. "We already know there are too many of them for us to take on."

"If it's going to take an hour or two for all of them to move past us, I don't want to sit here and count bodies. I want to find out roughly how many there are, and then I want to get to a place where I can transmit a quick report. Maybe the people back at the base can call in an air strike and knock them out while they're all together like this. If we wait too long, maybe they'll break up into smaller groups again."

"I've never seen this many of them at one time," said Richard.

"None of us have," said Cris. "That's what bothers me."

When Tony reached the base of the big oak, he reached down and manipulated the switches that released his legs from his upper body. Unlike those of most CCs, his was a special body, an "S" model, designed so that the upper portion could be interchanged with a variety of lower sections. It was also possible for Tony to function without any leg units at all, a tactic he had used many times in the past.

Now, by detaching his legs and leaving them behind, he could reduce his weight and thereby enable himself to get higher into the tree. His arms, which had more gripping and lifting power than a normal human's, could easily pull his torso up the trunk and onto the branches.

He began to climb, being very cautious. He wasn't too afraid of making noise, because at this time of year the tree didn't yet have leaves that would rustle if they were disturbed. But he was concerned about being visible to the xenoborgs if he ventured too far up, where the branches were thinner and less dense. As it turned out, his concern was needless.

Tony was fifteen feet off the ground when he grabbed for a branch that was about four inches in diameter. It should have supported his weight easily — but it was partially rotted away next to the trunk, on the side Tony couldn't see. When he curled his fingers around it and released his other hand to pull himself up, the branch gave way with a sharp crack. Tony and the branch came crashing down, snapping a few other small branches on the descent.

When he heard the noise, Cris froze. It seemed as loud as a gunshot in the still air, and he knew there was no way the xenoborgs could not have heard it as well. Yes — within about two seconds after the sound reverberated through the air, several of the monsters had raised the fronts of their bodies and turned their snouts toward the source of the noise. As that happened, he could hear more commotion coming from behind him — the sound of Tony scrambling back to where he had left his leg units, not bothering to be especially quiet about it.

Cris was ready to turn and run, positive that the monsters would waste no time in coming to investigate or, worse yet, simply blasting the grove of trees with all their firepower. Richard was already standing and half turned toward the far side of the grove, ready to take off at an instant's notice. As Cris started to turn and rise out of his crouch, he felt Maura's hand on his arm.

"Wait, Cris. Look."

It was inconceivable, but it was happening. Even the xenoborgs that had reacted to the sound had continued to move south all the while, keeping pace with the others ahead and behind them. And now they were all lowering their snouts and straightening out their bodies again, just as though nothing had happened, or as though what had happened was not important.

"I can't believe it," he whispered, half fearing

that at any second the monsters were going to pull out weapons and start cutting down the trees with everything they had. But from all appearances they had nothing of the sort in mind.

"It was an accident!" Tony said in a loud whisper as he rushed up behind Cris. "What do we do now?" he asked in a near panic.

"Nothing."

"Nothing?" Tony echoed, gazing out at the line of xenoborgs. "Didn't they hear it?"

"I'm sure they did," Cris answered. "But they don't seem to care."

The last xenoborg came trundling over the top of the slope about a minute later. Everyone had lost count of the exact number in the excitement, but the total was around fifty — the largest group of xenoborgs ever seen outside of a large city.

In light of what had happened in the meantime, Cris was not concerned in the least about not having an exact count to include in his report. How many there were no longer seemed important. The vital fact was that, for a reason he couldn't fathom, he and his fellow cyborg teammates would survive to make the report.

About fifteen minutes later the last of the xenoborgs disappeared out of sight to the south. It took a while longer for the four of them to calm down after their narrow escape, but once they did, the cyborgs felt the need to talk about it.

"Whew! I don't think I ever want to see that

many monsters in one place at once ever again!" Maura said, drowning out Cris's expression of utter disbelief.

"Sooo, this is what heaven looks like, eh? I could swear it looks a hell of a lot like the trampled earth I must have just been dispatched from," Tony said in his customary way of trying to cover up near-disaster with a joke.

"You keep talking like that and you'll get sent to the same place I imagine bad xenoborgs go!" Maura laughed.

"Where do bad xenoborgs go?" Tony asked, with feigned innocence.

"I'm not sure, but I don't think any of us would be very comfortable there," Maura said, stifling the urge to shudder.

The only cyborg who didn't seem to be able to ease his tension was Richard, who sat quietly while the others joked. It didn't take Cris, Maura, and Tony long to notice his silence.

"Hey buddy, you aren't going to let a few marching insects get you down, are you?" Tony asked, folding his frame down next to Richard's.

"Please, just leave me alone," Richard answered inoffensively.

"Sorry, Dick, old pal. I'm afraid I don't leave friends alone when they need someone to lean on," Tony said stubbornly.

"Me either," Cris said as he and Maura joined the other two.

"We aren't trying to be insensitive, Richard. We all know how you feel—" Maura's words were cut off by an angry barrage from Richard.

"No you don't, damn it!" he said, his voice choked with emotion.

"Then suppose you tell us how you feel," Cris urged gently.

"Look, I'm sorry," Richard apologized, his voice more controlled this time. "I don't mean to be rude. You've all been very pleasant to me. But I have some things that I just can't deal with, and seeing so many of those . . . those inhuman bastards just brought back a few unpleasant memories," Richard sputtered.

"I think we can all understand that," Maura tried again, this time getting a softer response from Richard.

"No offense, Maura, really," Richard said sincerely. "But how could either you *or* Cris understand how I feel? You both have each other. I have . . . no one." His words sounded more like a statement of fact than self-pity.

"Hey, pal, you've got me, and considering that cyborg females aren't exactly functional, if you know what I mean — no offense to present company, of course — what more could a lonely cyborg want?" Tony's words were meant to cause some lightheartedness on Richard's part, but the attempt didn't work.

"I appreciate your efforts, really. But I just have

to work this out by myself," Richard said with a tone of resignation.

"No you don't, damn it!" This time Tony's voice was anything but gentle. "We took you in and accepted you as our friend, and you let us. Once you did that, you gave up all rights to working anything out alone. We've all told you our stories, and now it's time for you to spill your guts!"

"He's right, Corporal W-105. We don't let our teammates suffer in silence," Cris said encouragingly.

"This doesn't happen very often, but I agree with Tony," Maura said.

"Come on, pal, what nightmare are you carrying around inside that brain capsule?" Tony coaxed.

Richard was silent for what seemed like a long while. The others waited patiently and were finally rewarded as he began to speak. His story, though initially not that different from thousands of others, made a definite impression on the three cyborgs who sat listening sympathetically — one that would stay with them the rest of their lives.

* * *

"I was stationed at Fort Sheridan, near Chicago, at the time of the invasion," Richard began, his voice a little shaky.

"Chicago — wasn't that one of the areas hardest hit by the aliens?" Cris asked.

"*The* hardest, from where I sit," Richard said seriously. "Anyway, the three of us, my wife—"

"You have a wife?" Tony asked, surprised that Richard hadn't mentioned her before now.

"Come on, guys. Quit interrupting him," Maura said. Realizing how hard it was for Richard to even begin talking, she didn't want him to keep getting stopped.

"Thanks, Maura," Richard said, his appreciation evident in his tone. "It is harder to get it out in short bursts. I'd rather just talk. . . ."

"Sorry. Go on, pal. We'll keep our mouths shut," Tony said.

"In answer to your question, Tony, I *had* a wife. Jacquie. She was beautiful. She's dead now." Richard was silent for a few seconds, and then he continued.

"Jacquie, our five-year-old daughter Danielle, and I were sleeping in our apartment on the base when we woke up to the sound of glass breaking and wood splintering. Danny was screaming and so, naturally, Jacquie and I both took off for her bedroom immediately.

"When we got there she was sitting up in bed, pointing at her window. What I saw breaking its way through the frame was worse than the worst nightmare imaginable." Richard shuddered visibly, and Tony reached out and put his hand on the cyborg's arm.

"Of course, it was one of the aliens, but at the

time none of us knew these things existed. And I found myself wondering if I was still asleep in my room dreaming. Anyway, I hesitated. . . . I should have *done* something instead of just standing there." Richard choked back a sob and took a deep breath before he continued.

"The creature wrapped two of its tentacles around my baby and dragged her screaming through the window. The last thing I ever heard her say was, "Help me, Daddy." At that point Richard's voice trembled and he broke down.

"I'm so sorry, Richard. Those bastards have caused more grief than I think any of us realize," Cris said sympathetically.

"What happened after your little girl was lost?" Maura asked, not meaning to be insensitive, but rather wanting to give Richard a chance to get it all out. And she knew there had to be more.

Richard took a few moments to pull himself together and then cleared his throat and continued his story.

"Jacquie just stood there screaming, in total shock over what had just happened. I left her there and raced through the apartment and out the door, hoping to stop whatever it was from dragging my daughter off to God only knows where! But when I got out there . . . God!"

Again Richard stopped talking, and this time Maura sat down beside him and put her arms around him.

"It's all right," she said soothingly. "Go ahead and cry all you want. It must have been awful."

"Oh, it was!" Richard cried, his sorrow turning to anger as he continued to speak. "There were three of them . . . and they were pulling her apart! By the time I got out there — I just can't stand to think of her having died like that!"

"Who could, friend?" Tony said gently, feeling sympathy and sadness well up inside him. "No one deserves to die that way, least of all an innocent child."

"She was so beautiful," Richard said pitifully. "So soft, so sweet, so innocent. And there she was, being ripped apart and chewed to pieces while I stood there helpless." He paused for a few seconds and then continued, this time his voice quieter, more controlled.

"Jacquie had pulled herself together enough to run to the window. In her shock and grief she must have thought she could do some good. Anyway, she started screaming at the monsters to let Danny go. It was too late for Danny, of course, but Jacquie didn't seem to notice. She just leaned out the window and screamed at the things, calling them names and telling them to let Danny go." Richard's voice grew softer. "I don't think she even realized what happened when one of the creatures reached in and got her. It was all over so quickly. And I just . . . I just stood there and watched."

All four cyborgs sat in silence for a while, three

of them doing so as a gesture of respect on Richard's behalf. Then Tony spoke.

"How did you manage to get away?" he asked, hoping to get Richard's mind off the grisly details of his wife's and daughter's deaths.

"I didn't," Richard said simply.

"What do you mean? You're here," Cris said, puzzled.

"I mean, they got hold of me and ripped me apart. The body you see is the only one I've got."

13

March 24-25, 2037

"I'm hungry, Daddy." Ryan's quiet statement, accompanied by a tug on Dan's sleeve, brought his father's troubled thoughts to an abrupt halt.

"I am too, guy. Maybe we'll find something at the next place we stop," Dan said comfortingly, although he was beginning to wonder if they would find anything to eat before the car ran out of fuel. There had been plenty of empty houses along the old country roads the group had spent most of the last twelve hours traveling. But they had all been ransacked, presumably by people in similar positions to the one shared by the seven people cramped in the compact car. Whatever food or fuel there might have been to be found had been taken already.

They had been following the same, pre-established procedure at every stop. Jerry would remain in the back seat, ready to restrain the still-distraught Kirk if that became necessary, while Suzie stayed in the front, assuming responsibility for Ryan and Jacob. Karen took Dan's place in the driver's seat while Dan got out, gun in hand, to search each of the places they came across, always cautious in case any of the monsters happened to be hiding within. And practically every time the end result was the same: no food, no fuel.

They would have spent some time in a few of the houses if there had been anything to eat. But nourishment was becoming crucial, especially considering that the group included a nursing mother with a baby who was obviously hungry.

Jacob had finally dropped into an exhausted sleep a few minutes earlier, but before that he had cried for almost three solid hours, causing his fellow passengers more than a little distress.

As the overloaded car reached the crest of a fairly steep hill, a large building came into view. Although they were still too far away to be able to tell whether it was a house, barn, or whatever, it was a safe bet that another farmhouse was there for the searching. "Oh, boy! This one's got to have something to eat!" Ryan cried with youthful optimism as the car closed the distance between them and what now appeared to be a large red frame house.

"Don't get your hopes up, guy," Dan cautioned his small son, hoping his use of the boy's favorite nickname would keep the warning from sounding as cruel as the words that followed. "All we've found to chew on in any of the other places has been some chipped paint or torn wallpaper. I really don't know if this time will be any different from the others."

"I could eat enough wallpaper to cover a whole house right now!" Ryan said enthusiastically and then added, "But don't worry, I'll save you all a few pieces."

Dan gave Ryan an appreciative grin. Just as he often purposely said things with the intention of cheering up his small son, Ryan had picked up the habit of doing the same for his father. Dan felt his eyes begin to fill with moisture as he thought about the kind of world in which he and Sharon had hoped to bring up their son. But instead of a stable, loving environment, one that included two parents, maybe a sibling or two, educational opportunities, and all the creature comforts of a normal, middle-class existence, the child had witnessed his mother's death and was now forced to spend his days trying to stay ahead of the unearthly creatures that had taken over the world.

The only education he was getting was how to stay alive for as long as possible, knowing that eventually they would bear down and put an end to the chase. Right now the boy was probably wondering if he'd ever eat again, but all he ever expressed were the simple words "I'm hungry." And when he did let those words slip, he always seemed to catch himself, with a maturity beyond his years, and not continue to dwell on it. Ryan had never been a complainer or a whiner. But if he chose to take up the habit at this stage of his young life, Dan would certainly understand why. And the fact that he not only refrained from complaining, but also had the unselfish sensitivity to try to make a joke out of a desperate situation, made Dan very proud indeed.

"Mommy was always very proud of you, guy, but if she could see you now, she'd be overwhelmed," Dan said quietly, placing his right hand on the child's knee and giving it a slight squeeze.

"I keep thinking about how she'd want me to be. And I know she'd tell me to take care of you, Daddy. She'd be proud of both of us, I think," Ryan said and then, in a voice that cracked with emotion, the child added, "I miss her so much, Daddy!"

"Me too, guy. Me too," Dan said. Then, more to himself than to his son, he added softly, "I wish to hell I could bring her back."

The car approached the gravel crossroad that led to the red house. Dan turned the vehicle to the right and announced to his passengers, his tone full of forced cheer, "Next stop, Grandma's House. Hope she's baked us a pie."

"Hell, I hope she's at least left us the apples to

go in it. I'll bake the damn pie myself!" Jerry said, also trying to sound a lot more lighthearted than he felt.

"If there *are* any apples in that house, I'm afraid they won't last long enough for anyone to use them for pie. Ryan and I intend to chow down the minute we see anything edible. Right, guy?" Karen asked, leaning forward and ruffling Ryan's straggly blond locks.

"Right!" he agreed enthusiastically, and then added, "Core and all!"

"My grandma used to bake apple pies," Kirk said quietly, startling his traveling companions. Other than his occasional crying jags and muttering how he had killed his grandmother, the boy hadn't verbalized anything in the days since the group had left the schoolyard. And he hadn't made any sound at all for a few hours.

"I'm sure she did, Kirk," Karen said gently.

"Not that I cared what they tasted like," Kirk continued, as though he hadn't heard Karen's remark. "The last time I really noticed much of anything my grandma did for me was when I was about Ryan's age. After that I never much appreciated having a grandmother, until—" A choked sob forced him to break off in mid-sentence.

"Kirk, please listen to me," Karen said, taking the boy's hand in hers. "You didn't cause your grandma's death. You had no way of knowing she'd come back and get caught by one of those creatures. You weren't thinking right at the time, and that's not your fault. No one can be blamed for not being able to deal with the terrible things that have happened. A lot of people have given up, and no one can blame them.

"You just wanted to give up because you couldn't deal with it any more. I'm sure your grandma understood that. She wouldn't have come back if she hadn't cared. And maybe it was all meant to work out the way it did. Your grandma's at peace right now. What you can do for her now is to take care of yourself and survive to see a better day." Kirk seemed to be listening intently as Karen spoke, but he didn't speak when she had finished.

Dan stopped the car in the driveway about twenty yards away from the battered farmhouse, then turned it around so that the vehicle was facing away from the building. While the others looked out the back and side windows, Dan pushed the horn button a few times to advertise their presence to anyone or anything that might be inside. If any people showed themselves and didn't seem threatening, the travelers would know it was safe to approach. If the horn attracted the attention of any monsters or any people who didn't seem inclined to help, Dan would step on the accelerator and get going in the opposite direction as quickly as possible.

When no one came to the door of the house within a couple of minutes, Dan and Karen got out of the car. Karen walked briskly around the side of the vehicle and eased herself into the driver's seat. She closed the door and immediately pushed the button that automatically locked all of the car doors. If something happened to Dan and the group had to leave in a hurry, they were all set to go — without him.

With the preliminaries taken care of, next came the hardest part for those in the car — the waiting.

As in previous "house raids," Dan first had to scout around the perimeter of the place to be sure there were no hostile elements within. Once he had established that the place was apparently deserted, he gave an "all clear" signal to those in the car and then went in to look around for food and drink.

Even after Dan disappeared inside the house, no one was optimistic; they had been disappointed too many times in the last few days. Their last success of any sort had been three days ago, when they came across an abandoned house that had running water from a still-functioning well. Dan had called Karen and Ryan inside to help fill as many containers as they could find. They took as much water as they could carry, but had to move on because they also needed food. And that was becoming harder and harder to find. At most of their stops, Dan had emerged holding out his hands, palms held upward in a gesture of emptiness.

This time was different.

"Eureka!" Dan yelled as he came bouncing down the crumbling stone steps leading to the front door several minutes after he had entered the house. Those waiting in the car cheered. Although they didn't know what was causing his elation, they had a fairly good idea that Dan had found something edible inside.

"Everyone get out and go inside!" he ordered happily. "We're gonna feast tonight!" With that the tired and hungry travelers wasted no time scrambling out of the car and hurrying toward the house.

"Wow!" Ryan exclaimed when Dan somewhat ceremoniously pulled open the pantry door.

"Grandma sure does know how to put up those veggies!" Jerry laughed, picking up a jar of canned string beans.

"When's supper?" Ryan asked eagerly.

"Soon, guy," Dan said. "But first we'd better load up the trunk with some of this stuff in case we have to leave in a hurry."

"Right!" Karen agreed. "And I think someone should check to see if there's a fuel tank on the property. We're running extremely low."

The group had left the Delavan area with the fuel tank three quarters full, and on two occasions had been able to siphon fuel from abandoned vehicles. They had not used the car any more than necessary in the last few days, but had been forced to keep moving recently in their search for food, and now their ability to stay on the move would be severely hampered unless they found a way to replenish the car.

"Let me look for the fuel." Kirk surprised everyone with those quietly uttered words. The others had been encouraged when he left the vehicle — the first time since his grandmother's death that he had moved without having to be prodded along. That had been one breakthrough — and now, almost on top of it, was another.

Jerry, who had been staying with the boy since he had reached for the door handle, guarding against anything foolish he might try to do, put his hand on Kirk's shoulder. "Are you sure you're all right?" he asked, looking intently into the young man's eyes for some sign of disturbance.

"No, I'm not. Not yet," Kirk answered slowly and sincerely. "But I intend to be. I want to stick around until I can figure out some way to pay those bastards back for what they did to my family."

"We all know that feeling," Dan said quietly.

"Yeah," Ryan agreed, walking over and taking Kirk's hand. "When I grow up, I'm going to stomp all over those things!"

"Well, right now we'd better get a move on so you can get something into that stomach of yours, or you won't be doing any growing!" Dan said, playfully mussing Ryan's hair.

"Okay. Come on, Kirk. Let's go see if we can scare up some fuel," Jerry said enthusiastically.

"Just make sure that's *all* you scare up!" Karen said playfully as Jerry and Kirk turned to leave the room.

"Don't worry," Jerry tossed back.

It took about ten minutes to clear the pantry of most of its edible contents — about the same amount of time it took Jerry and Kirk to establish that the only fuel tank on the premises contained nothing but air.

"Oh, well," Suzie said cheerfully as she mixed a pitcher of powdered milk with some of the water they had been carrying. "Maybe our luck will hold out and the next place we come to will have as much fuel as this one did food."

"It had better, or we'll be walking soon," Jerry said seriously.

Just then Ryan came bursting into the room to alert them that the food was ready. "Time to eat, everybody!" he announced grandly as he came through the door. There was no way of heating up a meal inside the house, since all the gas and electricity had long since been cut off in this area. So the cooking was done outside over a hastily built fire. In order to minimize the risk of the flames attracting wandering monsters, the food was cooked until it was barely warm and then the fire was immediately extinguished.

Karen moaned with pleasure as she savored the last of her red beets. As with the others, it had taken her no time at all to finish off a feast of string beans, beets, pickles, peaches, carrots, and powdered milk. Dan and Jerry had found a stash of beer, wine, and soda pop in the cellar, too. They had put most of that in the trunk, along with the rest of the food, but had left enough out to enjoy an evening of pleasure.

"Warm beer has never been one of my favorite things," Suzie said sarcastically as she took a sip of milk.

"You should try some — it might help you produce more milk," Karen suggested.

"Might help make Jacob a little tipsy, too," Suzie answered seriously.

"Or tired," Jerry added, his eyes twinkling mischievously.

"Tired — I like that idea! Let's keep lots of beer in the car!" Ryan exclaimed. "I'm almost deaf from that kid's screaming!" He screwed up his face so comically that everyone in the room began laughing.

"Don't feel bad, Ryan. You may have been sitting next to him, but *I* was holding him! I barely have any hearing left myself," Suzie said with mock seriousness.

"Oh, I'm really sorry," Ryan exclaimed, giving the woman a look of profound pity.

"What? I didn't hear that," Karen teased.

"I said . . ." Ryan raised his voice several notches and then muttered "Ohhh," when he realized he'd been tricked.

"Fooled him, didn't we, Jacob?" Suzie said with a laugh. She reached over and patted the baby as he lay on a stuffed, oversized chair she had pulled up beside her.

They were gathered around the solid pine table in the formal dining room of the pleasant country home, and for the moment at least, there was a feeling of normalcy. From all appearances, they could have been a normal family gathered together for an evening meal after a hard day of working the fields. And, almost as if to promote that illusion, Ryan asked innocently, "Can I go outside and play on the swing set, Dad?"

"No!" Dan's answer came out in a much sharper tone than he had meant, and he hastened to try to make up for snapping at the child. "I'm sorry, guy. I didn't mean to sound so rough. I just don't want you outside any more than you have to be. It's not safe."

"That's okay, Daddy. I understand. It seems so safe here that I forgot for a minute that those things are even out there. I really wish they'd go away." Ryan's voice faltered a little as he vehemently spewed out the last several words.

"We'll make them go away some day, Ryan. Don't worry," Karen said gently.

"For the moment, do you think we could make you go upstairs to the bedroom with all the games and miniature cars and play for a while before bedtime?" Dan asked with a sly grin on his face.

"Games? Cars? Wow!" Ryan nearly squealed with delight as he raced out of the room, returning a few seconds later to ask, "Where do I find the stairway?"

"Now there's a chip off the old block if I've ever seen one!" Dan said with a laugh as he got up from the table and led the eager child out of the room.

"I think I'll go see what's up there myself," Kirk said, pushing his chair back from the table and getting to his feet.

"Are you sure you're okay?" Jerry asked softly.

"I'm not going to do anything stupid, if that's what you mean," Kirk answered inoffensively. "I just thought maybe the kid could use a big brother to play with." And with that he turned and left the room.

"It must be so hard for him," Suzie said quietly after Kirk was gone.

"Yeah. And for Dan and Ryan, too. I don't know how either he or the kid manages to keep it together," Jerry agreed, and then gulped down the rest of his beer.

"Hey, take it easy there, sport," Suzie warned. "It's your night for diaper duty."

"You know," Karen said slowly, thoughtfully, "I really wouldn't mind keeping Jacob with me tonight. This would be a good opportunity for the two of you to spend some time together."

"That would be very nice," Suzie said enthusiastically.

"Yeah!" Jerry agreed without prompting.

"But we really couldn't ask you to give up your sleep," Suzie said firmly. She was torn between declining the offer out of consideration for Karen and taking advantage of it for her and Jerry's sake.

"No, I guess we couldn't," Jerry agreed, obviously disappointed. A quizzical look from his wife caused him to add a quick, "I mean, we wouldn't want to impose." He was having trouble figuring out what direction the conversation was taking.

Karen could see the confusion in Jerry's expression and the indecisiveness in Suzie's, and she stifled the urge to giggle. "Come on, you guys. Cut the bullshit. I know you could stand a break from the pleasures of parenting, and I think I'd have fun being a mommy for a while. And I *promise* I won't give him any beer!"

"It sure sounds like a good deal to me," Jerry said, giving Suzie a hopeful look.

"Well, if you're sure you really want to—" Suzie began, but was quickly cut off by Karen.

"I'm sure. Just tell me when to feed him and . . . uh, oh!" Karen stopped, laughing self-consciously as she realized she couldn't fulfill that part of being a parent.

"If he gets hungry, just bring him to Ms. Sustenance here. That's one thing only she can do," Jerry said, winking and pointing a thumb in the direction of his wife.

"Right," Karen agreed and then got up and

picked Jacob up off of the chair. "Hey, Spud, it's just you and me tonight. So how about giving Aunt Karen a break and not doing any of those messy little numbers in your diaper until tomorrow morning, okay?" Karen cooed, gently rocking the baby back and forth in her arms.

"Maybe we should get out of here while the getting's good," Jerry said as he pushed his chair back. He stood up and extended a hand toward Suzie in a gesture of gallantry.

"No argument from this end," Suzie said, standing up and taking her husband's hand.

Dan came back into the dining room as Jerry and Suzie were on their way out. "Call me when it's my turn to take over watching," Jerry called back over his shoulder, adding, "But knock first, okay?"

"Knock where?" Dan asked, wondering what was going on.

"Wherever you find a room with a locked door," Suzie answered, and then the two were out of sight, their muffled giggles fading away soon after.

"What's that all about?" Dan asked, sitting down at the table next to where Karen sat holding Jacob.

"Love," she said simply, and then added, "Do you remember?"

"Too well," Dan sighed, giving her a thoughtful look. "You haven't said much about your husband," he prompted gently.

"There really isn't a whole lot for me to say. We

weren't like you and Ryan's mother," Karen answered sadly.

"But you must miss him," Dan said, wondering how she managed to deal with her grief so well.

"No," she said, holding Jacob closer to her. "Other than the fact that I feel bad for him, I can't say I'm sorry he's dead."

"How can you say that? I can't imagine ever being glad that Sharon died!" he said incredulously. "I don't think there'll ever come a time when I stop missing her."

"If Tom had been anything like you or Jerry, I'd be crying, at least on the inside, right now. But the fact is, he wasn't a very nice man, to put it mildly. And I have the scars to prove it." There was no hint of self-pity in her voice. She was merely offering a straightforward account of how things stood.

"I'm really sorry," Dan said as he reached out and put his hand on Karen's arm. "I can be such a jerk sometimes!"

"It's not your fault. You had a good marriage. You lost a woman you really loved, and who, I'm sure, really loved you. Our situations were just different . . . much different," Karen said gently.

"Well, they certainly aren't much different any more, are they?" Dan said softly, hoping to bridge the gap he thought he'd caused.

"Nope, except that tonight you're on bug patrol and I'm on baby patrol!" Karen responded, winking.

"I'll trade you," Dan said, holding out his arms.

"Oh, no you don't! I don't make unfair trades. I will, however, allow you to hold my cuddly little charge while I hunt up something to use for a diaper. The way he smells right now, I doubt if even one of those monsters would come near him!" she said, handing the baby over to Dan's waiting arms.

"Oh sure, *now* you're willing to give him up!" Dan said teasingly, and then almost gagged when he got a whiff of the baby's handiwork. "Hurry!" he called after Karen as she disappeared out the door.

Dan got up out of his chair and walked across the room and into the kitchen. Since their arrival, the group of trespassers had made periodic checks on the area surrounding the house. There had been no sign of the ugly creatures, but Dan was not about to take any chances. If he saw any of the monsters coming their way, he wanted everyone to be in the car and on the road in a minute or less. He checked the kitchen windows, which faced south. He could see no sign of any activity outside.

Dan exited the kitchen through the doorway that led to the living room. This time he checked the windows facing north. All was quiet on that front, too.

"Okay, I got a diaper. Now you can change him," Karen said, innocently holding a swatch of cloth out for Dan to take.

"Me? I'm on bug patrol, remember?" Dan said,

placing Jacob down on the seat of the upholstered couch.

"But I thought you wanted to trade duties," Karen said with mock innocence.

"That was before I got a whiff of this kid! Whew! I didn't think *anything* smelled this bad!" Dan said overdramatically, making a gruesome face.

Karen laughed so hard she almost doubled over. When she was able to talk she said, "But surely you've done this sort of thing before. What did you do when Ryan pooed his pants?"

"Well, I uh, hmm," Dan said evasively.

"You let your wife change him, didn't you?" Karen asked accusingly.

"Well, she was usually the one he was around at the time of . . . Well, you know, when he 'pooed' — as you so crudely put it," Dan said defensively.

"You mean there was never a time when Ryan poo— I mean, *filled* his diapers, that you were with him and could have changed him if you'd had the nerve?" Karen pressed.

"I had plenty of nerve," Dan countered as he headed for the doorway. "I just didn't have the stomach for it. Still don't. So take your time. I'll be back in a while, when the room's aired out!"

* * *

Dan had been asleep for three hours when Karen woke him. At first he wasn't sure what was happening. He remembered he had put Ryan to bed and then stood watch until two in the morning. Karen had put Jacob down, and she had kept Dan company until Jerry came on duty. Then, presumably, she had gone to bed too. But she was here now, frantically trying to get him up.

"Dan, please!" Her tone was desperate. "You have to wake up!"

Dan regained consciousness suddenly and sat bolt upright in bed. "What? What is it?" he asked, trying to shake the cobwebs from his brain. He noticed through the window the faint glow of dawn in the eastern sky.

"Oh, Dan, there are lots of them! And they're coming this way!" Karen almost sobbed. And suddenly, Dan was very wide awake.

14

March 25, 2037

Its hunger having been satisfied for the time being, the Master surveyed the situation on planet Earth and found that to be also satisfactory.

All that was required to get the xenoborgs to begin congregating was to stop sending out any other instructions. They were communal creatures by nature, so, in the absence of orders to the contrary, they simply — stupidly — turned away from what they were doing and pointed themselves in the direction of the nearest large group of their own kind.

The Master was elated at the simplicity of that part of Its plan. Never before had It accomplished so much by doing nothing at all.

But It would not remain idle in the meantime. While the xenoborgs gathered for the final assault there was a bit more work to do — work that It welcomed because It, like any super-intelligent being, enjoyed mental activity.

The tactic It was about to employ had never been used before, because every other time the Master had conquered a world, It had done so with the intent of putting the world to use when the battle was over. This time, that was no longer a consideration.

The humans had put up a system to keep Its transport vessels from approaching, but that defense system could not guard against what It would now rain down on the planet from the void beyond Earth's atmosphere: radiation, collected into receptacles and then focused on selected locations and delivered in short, concentrated doses. Radiation that would not harm human beings . . . directly.

Radiation that would be difficult to detect, considering the current abysmal state of man's technology, and even if detected would be impossible for the humans to deflect or neutralize in time. Radiation that would, in a matter of Earth days, mutate some of the lowest life forms on the planet into creatures that It could control — creatures that It would use as instruments of annihilation. By the time the xenoborgs had massed themselves into the hordes that would serve as the vanguard for the final offensive, they would be joined by millions of mindless allies.

In their natural state, the insects of Earth were remarkable creatures, performing feats of strength and acts of destruction that seemed far beyond the abilities of organisms that were so tiny, so frail. When they were mutated into creatures hundreds of times larger than normal and sent forth on an organized plan of devastation, just think what they could do. . . .

The Master allowed Itself a few moments of contemplation as It did just that, visualizing horrified crowds of humanity fleeing before the march of a force that could not be stopped — a force that would leave nothing but rubble and death in its wake. With visible effort, It curbed Its glee; the elation It felt now would be multiplied many times over when Its expectations turned to reality.

It could hardly wait.

15

March 25, 2037

Karen had gone to bed about the same time as Dan, but Jacob woke up crying shortly afterward and she had been trying to soothe the unhappy baby ever since. He would drop off to sleep for a few minutes at a time, but then would stir and wake up again, as though he realized even in his sleep that he wasn't with his mother.

Finally, about 4:30 a.m., Karen gave up trying to keep Jacob pacified and knocked on the door of the room where Suzie was sleeping. A sleepy Suzie had come to the door and taken Jacob who, Karen told the tired mother, was probably hungry. Suzie thanked Karen and told her she would feed the baby and put him back to sleep.

Since she was up anyway and it was almost morning, Karen decided to keep Jerry company on sentry duty. They engaged in quiet, idle conversation as they made the rounds from one side of the house to the other, spending a couple of minutes looking out in one direction and then moving to a different vantage point. It was a lookout system that Dan had devised and passed on to Jerry when he roused him in the middle of the night to take over. The four walls of the house faced the cardinal directions, so by making a leisurely circuit of the downstairs windows every five or six minutes, one person could effectively keep an eye on all the terrain around the building.

As his time on sentry duty passed, Jerry became more and more secure. He realized from experience, as did anyone else who had managed to survive this long, that the monsters were not nearly as mobile and aggressive at night as they were in daylight. And because the farmhouse was situated on flat terrain, he had a view for at least a half-mile in any direction. He also knew that although the creatures were vicious, they were not especially fast. Even if one or more of them appeared on the eastern horizon, for instance, just after he turned away from looking in that direction, he would make his circuit and return to the east windows in time to spot them when they were still a long distance away.

All of that was sound reasoning in normal circumstances. But what happened at the crack of dawn on this day was not normal.

The first rays of the rising sun radiated out over the eastern horizon as Jerry and Karen peered dutifully through the windows facing north. "Another new day," Jerry muttered softly.

"Thank God for that," Karen responded, reading his tone of voice correctly. For seven people who were constantly on the run, who usually didn't know where their next meal or their next gallon of fuel was coming from, every sunrise was a victory of sorts. The dawn signaled the end of yet another day through which they had survived . . . and, she thought despondently, the beginning of another day of struggling and desperation — another day that might be the last for any or all of them.

They moved to the west windows, then the south, then the east, each time keeping a vigil for somewhere between two and three minutes before moving on. The sky was clear, and by the time they returned to the east windows the sun had risen enough so that Jerry and Karen had a hard time looking directly at it. As they moved to the north side of the house, Karen momentarily had trouble adjusting her eyes to the change in illumination.

At first when she gazed to the north, she had trouble seeing anything at all. Then, as her vision cleared, she couldn't believe her eyes.

In the minutes since they had last scanned this direction, a long line of monsters had seemingly appeared out of nowhere. Without consciously counting, she knew there were at least a dozen in sight. And even as she watched for no more than a few agonizing seconds, they came visibly closer and another creature came into view on the horizon. They were moving right down the center of the road that ran past the house, at a pace that would bring them close to the building in only a few minutes.

Jerry and Karen snapped out of their shock at the same time, and without exchanging words both of them knew what to do. They took off in different directions and ran through the house sounding an alarm. Within minutes everyone had been roused and gathered in the living room. As soon as Dan fully understood the situation and realized it would be fruitless to try escaping in the car, he ordered everyone down into the basement. A small window on the north side of the room at ground level enabled them to get a continuing look at the line of monsters. The creatures moved in single file like a parade of troops passing in review. They shuffled right down the middle of the road as though they owned it, as though daring anyone to try to take it away from them.

"Are they going to eat us now, Daddy?" Ryan asked, his voice shaky and weak.

"No!" Dan said. "I won't let them." The usual response, he said to himself. But how much longer could he keep the monsters from "eating us" if that was what they wanted to do? And how much longer would Ryan continue to take his empty reassurances at face value? The boy was no dummy, and he was getting older and wiser all the time.

"Actually, I'm not sure they can get at us as long as we stay down here," Karen contributed. "The only problem is, we left all the food upstairs. So if they . . ." She didn't finish that thought. She didn't need to. If the monsters chose to investigate the house, they would almost certainly find and consume or destroy the food. And it was entirely possible that if they also decided to flatten the house where it stood, the basement would become a tomb for everyone in it. Dan considered those possibilities, and as they ran through his mind he found himself rationalizing that suffocation or starvation was preferable to being mangled or eaten alive.

Then he stopped himself, and in the next few seconds a great change came over Dan Murphy. What am I doing? he asked himself. Hiding here like a trapped rat, making value judgments about the way I'd prefer to die. . . .

It's time to take control, he told himself. Time to think about living instead of dying. About fighting instead of running.

There was no getting around the trouble they were in at the moment. They *were* trapped, and it would be foolish if not suicidal to try escaping. But if they were still alive after the monsters had gone on their way, Dan vowed that he would find a way

— any way — to turn himself and the rest of these people from runners into fighters.

"What are we going to do?" The question came from Kirk, and it was delivered in a cool, even tone of voice that Dan had never before heard from the boy. He didn't sound panicky, and the question itself was evidence that he certainly wasn't fatalistic. He was looking to Dan for leadership, for a decision. Dan didn't fail to perceive that, and when he answered Kirk's question he spoke to the entire group.

"For now, not a thing," he said firmly. "We wait until they're gone — and then we go out there and start figuring out how to give those bastards what they deserve.

"I can't speak for the rest of you," he continued after a short pause, "but I've had it up to here with running and hiding. We can't go on living like this forever."

He stopped and moved over to the small window, where Karen had been keeping an eye on the procession. "They just keep coming," she said, successfully keeping the tremor out of her voice. "So far I don't think any of them have turned this way."

"Good," Dan said as he started to turn back toward the rest of the group again. Karen laid a hand on his forearm, and he stopped.

"I agree with you, Dan," she said with quiet determination. "I hate living in fear, wondering when and how the end will come. I don't want to die, but I think I could accept it if I could take at least one of those . . . things . . . with me."

Dan took her by the shoulders and looked in her eyes. What he saw there was sincerity, dead seriousness, and a glimmer of something else he hadn't seen in anyone's eyes since the day Sharon Murphy died. He brought her to him in a brief but tight embrace, then moved away from her slightly to receive Ryan when the boy came up and threw his arms around his father's stomach.

"I don't like being hungry all the time," he said. "And I'm tired of being afraid!" His voice rose in pitch as he added those words, and he seemed to be near tears, but it was also clear that he meant what he said.

"I think your son speaks for all of us," said Jerry. He looked at Suzie and then at Kirk after he spoke, and both of them nodded their heads.

"I love Jacob more than life itself," Suzie said, her voice shaking, "but I don't want to bring him up in this kind of a world. I'd rather . . ." She choked and broke down into soft sobbing as Jerry reached out to comfort her.

"I owe it to my family, especially my grandma," said Kirk. "She was the kind of person who would have gone down fighting if she'd had a chance, and I kept her from getting that chance. So now it's up to me to take her place."

Dan strode over to where Kirk was standing and

extended his right hand. The boy took it with his own and held it in a grip that caught Dan off guard with its strength. "We have a lot in common," Dan said. Kirk fixed Dan with a steely gaze, and when the boy responded Dan thought for an instant that he had lapsed back into anger and depression.

"Two days ago," Kirk began, "I would have punched you in the mouth for saying that. Today, I'll take it as a compliment." Then, for the first time any of them could remember, Kirk Christiansen smiled.

"Hey!" Karen interrupted. "I think I see the caboose!"

Dan, Kirk, and Jerry all moved to the window, jockeying so that all of them could see outside at the same time. Sure enough, they could see what appeared to be the last monster in the line. "We're not out of danger yet," said Dan, "but we should know where we stand within the next few minutes."

Because the basement had no windows facing any direction but north, the people inside couldn't follow the progress of the monsters along the highway and had no way of knowing if any of the creatures were turning to approach the house after moving out of their field of vision. All they could do, as they had done on so many other similar occasions, was wait . . . and hope.

The last monster in line shuffled out of sight, and still they waited. Nothing had happened, as far as they could tell, to disrupt the silence near the house. But they couldn't see most of the area outside — and for all they knew, they might emerge from the basement to the sight of several dozen monsters surrounding the place on the other three sides, ready to pounce as soon as some sign of activity became evident.

Finally, after interminable minutes during which none of the adults would bring up the subject, Ryan spoke.

"How long do we have to stay down here?" he asked his father. That was all it took.

"Just another couple of minutes," Dan said. Then, to the group, "Should be all clear by now. I'll go up and check."

"Let me," Kirk insisted, already moving toward the stairway. Before Dan could get out more than a syllable in response, he added, "I can *do* it."

"I was going to say, 'Go right ahead.' I know you can do it," Dan said. "Just go slowly, be quiet, and be careful."

Kirk was up the stairs — quickly, but quietly — in seconds. Half a minute later he reappeared, coming down the steps just far enough to announce, "Nothing out there as far as the eye can see — they're gone!"

* * *

"I can't believe how lucky we were," Jerry said as the group gathered in the kitchen.

"Let's consider it a good omen," Dan suggested. "And maybe some day soon, we'll have more to celebrate than the fact that we didn't get . . ." He let the rest of the thought go unspoken as he realized Ryan was within earshot.

"I know what you were going to say, Dad," Ryan told his father. "I'm not a baby any more."

"No, you're not — that's for sure," Dan said as he drew his son to him and hugged him. "Now," he continued in a businesslike tone, "we need a plan of action. Any suggestions?"

"I think we should stay here for another day at least," Suzie ventured as she tried to comfort Jacob, who was starting to fuss again. "We have food and shelter, and I think I'd be able to get Jacob to sleep longer if we could stay in one place for a while." Despite the respite Karen had given her during the previous night, she was clearly on the verge of exhaustion from having to tend to the infant almost constantly.

"I understand," Jerry said, directing his words to his wife, "and I wish you and Jacob didn't have to go through this. We do have food and shelter here, but we're also in a very vulnerable position. After what almost happened to us a while ago, I think we'd be better off staying on the move."

"I agree," Karen said. "We don't know how far away those creatures went. Maybe they have some kind of camp in the area, in which case I'd just as soon not stick around here."

"Let's take stock," said Dan. "We now have enough food to last us for a few days, if we conserve it. We have enough fuel in the tank to get fifty or sixty miles if we take it slow. And except for the parade we watched a while ago, it seems that the farther north we've gone the fewer monsters we've run across. I think we ought to head north, maybe try to make it to around Green Bay."

"And then what?" asked Kirk. "Try to cop some more fuel and just keep on moving?" The questions were matter-of-fact, not accusatory.

"No," said Dan, his jaw set in a hard line. "I meant what I said down in that basement, and I assume the rest of you did, too. Our first goal should be to get to a place where we *don't* have to keep running. Find a spot we can call home, get ourselves established, and then start coming up with ways to take the fight to these creatures. They must be vulnerable to something."

"I wish I knew what," Jerry said.

"Well," Karen chimed in brightly, "we're just going to have to figure something out, right?"

"Right!" echoed Ryan, and the others contributed their assent to that.

"I do declare!" said Dan in mock wonderment. "I believe that's the first time I've ever heard all of us agree on something!"

"Things are looking up," Karen said, catching his eye.

"You bet they are," Dan responded, returning

her warm look as he reached out to squeeze her hand.

* * *

This has been one hell of a lucky day for this family!" Dan said as he got back into the car after filling the fuel tank to the brim and tossing a couple of one-gallon containers in the trunk for good measure. After leaving the farmhouse, they had traveled north for all of fifteen minutes when they spotted a dwelling far off to the west, connected to the highway by a one-lane dirt road nearly a mile long.

They had decided on the spot that it was worth a try, and when they got to the place it turned out to be worth much more than that. The farmhouse was occupied by an elderly couple who greeted the group with open arms. After sharing a meal with their hosts, during which time they exchanged stories of the horde of creatures that had passed through the area earlier that day, the visitors had told the couple of their plans to keep heading north and Dan had asked if there was any place nearby to get fuel.

"Got plenty of it right here," Andrew Larson responded, allowing himself a smile as he saw the amazement on Dan's face. "Take all you want."

Dan could hardly believe their luck. But he was also concerned about Andrew and his wife, Helen.

"Is there enough for you, too, if you need it?" he asked seriously.

"Don't expect we'll be needin' it," Andrew answered quickly.

Helen went on to explain that she and her husband had long ago decided to live out their days on the family homestead — "Bugs or no bugs!" as she put it.

"Most o' the people who used t' live around here never got killed by the bugs — they just got panicky and took off," she said. "You've seen some o' the empty places, I reckon?" Dan nodded at that.

"Well," she went on in a pleasant tone, "we decided the first time we saw one o' those things that there wasn't any sense tryin' to run away. And what would we run to? We're too old, and too tired, and everything we care about is right here."

"I can appreciate that," Dan responded quietly.

"But you can't give up!" Kirk argued. "You can't just stay here and wait for them to come and—"

"Now listen!" said Andrew Larson in his low, gravelly voice. "Make no mistake — if I was young like you people I'd be out there fightin' even if all I had was my pitchfork and my bare knuckles!" To drive home that last point he balled his left hand into a fist and shook it beside his head. "If I did any runnin' at all, it would be at 'em, not away from 'em!" he finished angrily.

"I know what you're saying," Dan said quietly, "but as far as we've seen, normal people have absolutely no defense against those things out there. All we can do for now is try to stay one step ahead of them until—"

"That right there is the crux of the matter," Andrew interrupted, his head bobbing slowly up and down as if to lend credence to his words. "Those creatures out there have most people convinced that we can't do anything about 'em. So we hide and let some synthetic men do all of our work for us." Andrew was quiet for several seconds and then he added, almost bitterly, "We don't need any damn super-bodies to be able to fight these things. What we need is for people to realize they *can* do something, if they'd only come outta hiding long enough!"

The rest of the meal was spent in silence after that. When they were all finished eating, Helen led Dan and Karen out to the large holding tank that, the woman said, should have enough fuel to overflow a dozen automobile tanks. "We haven't used much since the last time we had this filled," Helen said "Car gave up an' died two winters ago — and we got no place t' go anyway."

While Dan and Karen put fuel in the car, the rest of their group helped clean up the kitchen and asked if there was anything they could do for the couple before they left.

"Well, I hate t' ask. . . ." Andrew said after a pause.

"Name it," Jerry said quickly.

"Since the pump went out we haven't had any running water. Helen has to get water from a stream about a half-mile from here. She can only carry a couple o' buckets, so she has to make lotsa trips back and forth. If you could each go get some water, so she can have a bit of a break . . ."

"Say no more!" Kirk said enthusiastically. "We'll flood this place!"

"Well, now, I don't know about that!" Andrew said with a chuckle.

By the time they were ready to leave, the visitors had gathered enough water to last the couple a week, for which Helen was almost tearfully grateful. "You have no idea how wonderful it's been to have guests. I sure do wish you all could stay."

"Who knows, we may just make it back this way," Karen said, giving the woman a spontaneous hug. "And if we do, you can count on us stopping."

"That would be wonderful," Helen said, her eyes filling with moisture. "Haven't had any kids around here for a long time."

* * *

The group traveled in silence for several minutes after getting out of sight of the Larsons' home. Kirk was the first to speak, and he put into words essentially what all of them had been thinking.

"What that old man said has been going around and around inside me," he said. "I really think he would fight with his bare hands if he could. And he's really got me talked into it. I feel like running up and beating the hell out of the next monster we see."

"I don't think there's a person alive who hasn't dreamed of doing just that," Jerry responded. "And I think we all feel the same way — about figuring out a way to fight instead of running and hiding for the rest of our lives. But I can't imagine how we could just stand up to them and trade blows. Cyborg Commandos are the only ones I know of who can do that and get away with it."

"Did you ever think of becoming a Cyborg Commando?" Kirk asked.

"Lots of times," Jerry answered without pausing. "But I wouldn't be able to take care of Suzie, and now Jacob, at the same time. I'm one of the few lucky ones who still has a family intact. I'm not about to desert them."

"I've thought about joining the program, too," Karen said. "When the aliens first came down, and Tom and I were on the run, I suggested it to him several times. We don't — didn't — have any children, and I thought we'd be perfect candidates. But he wouldn't even talk about it. Then I picked up with you guys and . . . well, shucks, I just haven't been able to tear myself away." She smiled as Ryan leaned his head against her arm.

"We wouldn't let you go anyway," the boy said.

"From what I've heard," Dan said to Karen,

"everybody who applies has to go through some heavy physical and psychological testing. From what you've told us about Tom, I don't think he'd have stood a chance in hell. He was nothing but bad news." Dan's voice was vehement, almost angry, by the time he finished. He was a little surprised — and embarrassed, too — by his reaction.

Neither Dan's words nor his tone of voice went unnoticed by Karen, but she didn't take offense. In fact, her reaction was quite the opposite. He hadn't come right out and said it, but Dan was clearly concerned about her. Concerned to the point of being protective of her and hostile toward a man he had never even known, and who wasn't even alive any more.

"Anyway," Kirk began, getting the conversation back on its original track, "Ryan, Jacob, and I are all too young to become CCs, so if we're gonna stay together then it looks like we'll have to figure out some other way to fight these things."

"Let's just keep thinking that way," Dan said. "Sooner or later we'll come up with an idea, or we'll run across an opportunity we haven't had before."

"Optimism!" said Jerry cheerily. "From now on we look ahead instead of over our shoulders. Right?"

"Right!" answered everyone else in unison, repeating the all-for-one vow they had first voiced a few hours earlier.

No one had anything to say for about ten minutes after that, until suddenly Dan and Karen both noticed two figures moving toward the road up ahead of the car.

"It looks like a couple of men waving at us to stop!" Karen exclaimed

"They're waving, all right!" Dan agreed. "But they sure as hell aren't men!"

16

March 25, 2037

Richard's last statement left his teammates in shock. As CCs, until the time of the first successful brain transplant reversal, they had lived with the knowledge that they might never again be able to go back to being normal human beings. But there had always been hope for them to cling to.

Richard had no such hope. His body had been mauled beyond recognition by the invading xenoborgs, and it was only because their attention was diverted elsewhere that Richard was finally, mercifully, left alone. By then there was barely any life left in the mutilated soldier.

He didn't remember any of it beyond the sound and the initial pain of being ripped to shreds. Richard had lapsed into unconsciousness shortly after an alien had ripped off one of his arms. All he knew about what had happened afterward was what he had been told by others.

"So how did you get away? How did you manage to survive?" Tony asked after about a minute of silence, feeling a new sense of respect for his fellow CC.

Richard had composed himself quite well by now and, having made it past the part about his wife and daughter, told the rest of his story with scarcely a break. "Apparently the invaders tore up the base pretty bad, and everyone was running around like crazy, trying to dodge or escape the creatures," Richard answered. "I was told that two of my friends, one of whom was one of the base medics, found me still alive, gathered up what was left of me, and got me out of the line of fire and into the underground complex on base."

"Your base had a CC center?" Cris asked.

"Yeah. I didn't know much about it before the invasion, only that it was there. I knew there was some intense research going on and that it had to do with creating some new breed of synthetic soldier," Richard paused and then continued. "There was a general information meeting aimed at recruiting volunteers — most of us called them guinea pigs — to help further the research. Anyone who was serious about volunteering for the program was given more information. I never pursued it. I didn't even tell Jacquie about it. I figured she'd never go for it.

"Anyway, I was taken underground and, from what I'm told, I was kept on life support for about six months before finally starting to come around. By then I had been evacuated, along with the rest of the personnel at the Chicago base who survived, and I was recovering in the medical facility attached to the CC secondary base in Holland, Michigan.

"It took another three months after that for me to get my bearings, mentally, and fully comprehend all that had happened to me. At first I was so full of drugs and so grief-stricken that I didn't notice how bad my physical condition really was. But as I became more aware, I became more alarmed about my almost total inability to function," Richard said.

"I could think, and I could see. But I couldn't talk. I couldn't move or feel anything below my chin. I thought maybe I was paralyzed. What I didn't know was that there was nothing but a few vital organs lying in that bed, and they were what kept me alive. All I really had left that was able to function on its own was my mind.

"I tried to take comfort in that, but as the days and weeks went by — very slowly — I grew restless and was almost crazy with the desire to feel or move or talk to someone. I cried incessantly, and I could see nothing but pity and compassion in the eyes of the people who took care of me.

"I wanted so much to tell them how I felt, to simply wish them a good morning or thank them for their kindness," Richard blurted emotionally, obviously distressed by the painful memories. He took a few seconds to collect himself before continuing. "They talked to me a lot. That's how I learned about what had happened. And that's how I learned about the CC program I had rejected earlier. It didn't take a whole lot of prompting for me to blink my eyes three times, the sign that they had told me to use for the word 'yes,' when I was asked if I wanted to undergo a brain transplant operation.

"Of course I wanted a new body! There was certainly no old body to worry about losing. And if my brain died during the operation, then it would be a welcome relief. I had nothing to lose and everything to gain," Richard concluded. He paused for a couple of beats and then added, his tone somewhat lighter now, "And here I am."

"Wow! In your case, you must not mind being stuck in this contraption the military calls a body!" Tony said.

"Not a bit," Richard said with conviction. "I can still remember what it was like to be a prisoner in my bed. I'm glad to have a body that can walk and run and hold onto things. I feel very lucky . . . in that respect."

"I imagine you had to overcome a lot of fear about xenoborgs, considering what you went through," Maura said sympathetically.

"No, as a matter of fact, I didn't," Richard said thoughtfully. "All I've felt for them since I regained consciousness is hatred and loathing. There's nothing more those creatures can do to Richard Adams. But there's one hell of a lot that Richard Adams intends to do to them!"

"And on that note," Cris said, getting to his feet, "we really should be letting the guys back at the base know what's going on out here." As Richard rose and stood beside him, Cris turned to address the corporal. "Richard, I don't know what else to say except that, although I'm very sorry about the circumstances that led to your decision to become a Cyborg Commando, I'm happy for our sakes that you did. You're shaping up to be one hell of a teammate — and a friend."

"Thanks, Cris," Richard said with heartfelt appreciation.

"So — what now, boss?" Tony asked. "Do we head for home?"

"No, you're going to stay here and be recruiters. Maura and I will head for that piece of high ground," Cris said, pointing toward a hill on the distant northern horizon, "and I'll dash off a radio message about the caravan before it gets too much farther away. See you in about an hour." With that, he and Maura strode away briskly.

"So what are you going to do when and if this thing ever ends?" Tony asked Richard as they sat back to back just inside the grove of trees watching for approaching people or vehicles.

"Well, when and if it's over, I figure they'll still

need some of us for other duties that require nearly indestructible bodies, so I guess I'll just stay in service until I die."

"I wonder what it would be like to be an old cyborg. . . . What happens when a CC gets senile?" Tony said, more to himself than to his companion.

"Gosh," said Richard in a sarcastic but light tone. "Thanks for giving me something to look forward to."

"Hey man, I'm sorry," said Tony, turning briefly to look at Richard. "I didn't mean—"

"Relax. No problem. I realized long ago that I was going to grow old in this body," Richard said quickly, trying to set his friend's mind at ease. Tony settled down and resumed his scanning to the south. "But I guess I never thought of it in geriatric terms. I suppose the military is going to have to arrange to have a few retirement homes built especially for aging CCs. I can see it now . . ."

Richard's musing came to an abrupt halt as Tony gave out a shout and sprang to his feet. He whirled to see the cause of Tony's excitement, and a second later was also up and moving, heading toward the highway — toward a small car coming at them from the south.

* * *

"I can't believe it," said Dan, a thin smile on his face.

"No, really," Tony said. "We *do* need you — you and anybody else we can find. We can do it, if—"

"That's not it," Dan interrupted. "I do believe there's a plan to beat the . . . what did you call them?"

"Xenoborgs," Richard supplied. "But you can just call them monsters."

"I've called them a few worse things than that in my time," Dan said gruffly. "What I meant was, we've just been talking about how we're sick of running away and hiding — sick of letting these . . . xenoborgs . . . do whatever they want. I was just saying how we should be on the lookout for an opportunity to fight them."

"Well, you've come to the right place," said Tony. "Wanna hear more?"

"You bet," said Kirk as a cold smile crossed his face.

"Okay, here's how it works. Some of the xenoborgs, the leaders, have built-in equipment just like we do — lasers, projectile weapons, sensors, communication devices. Those are the ones we've been having trouble with, because they're just about as powerful as we are, and there are a lot more of them than there are of us."

"But if you can't stand up to them," asked Dan, "how are we supposed to do that?"

"With all due respect, the sergeant is getting a little ahead of himself," Richard said. "The heart of the matter is this: Xenoborg weapons get their operating power from organisms that the creatures carry around inside them — some kind of animal that's able to store up electrical energy and release it later. We don't have to take on the leaders; all we have to do is deprive them of these power sources. Then, when their weapons and sensors go dead, we — the CCs — can cut them down."

"We're with you so far," said Jerry. "But if these electric-things are inside their bodies, how do we get at them? And how do we kill them?"

Tony picked up the explanation. "When the electric-things — we call them 'powwers' — start to run low, the xenoborgs have to take them out of their bodies for recharging. And the only way they can be recharged, as far as we know, is to dump them into a body of water and let them sit for a few hours soaking up sunlight."

"Solar batteries?" interjected Dan.

"Something like that," answered Richard. "The thing is, if they're removed from the water or if their source of light is cut off, then they can't recharge. They become useless, and then they die."

"I still don't see where we fit in," said Kirk, intrigued but puzzled.

"I'm sure the corporal intended to get around to that very soon," said Tony with a sidelong glance at Richard. "To keep the powwers from recharging, to pull them out of the water after they're dropped or to cover them so they can't get sunlight, we need lots of teams working at the same time. We need to put surveillance on any possible recharging site we can locate, wait for powwers to be dropped, and then move in with nets and tarpaulins — nets to haul them out of the water, tarps to throw over them and block the sunlight.

"Obviously, there aren't enough of us to cover all the lakes and streams — *that's* where you fit in. We give you the equipment, assign you to an area of responsibility, and you get to go fishing."

"It sounds too simple," said Dan. "What's the hitch?"

"It *is* simple," Tony responded. "That's why it has a good chance of working. But we're not trying to kid anyone. The 'hitch,' if that's what you want to call it, is that wherever you find a bunch of powwers, you can bet that a group of xenoborgs won't be far away. Not everyone who goes out fishing is going to catch something — and some people aren't going to live long enough to talk about the one that got away. Does that say it plainly enough?"

"Crystal clear," Dan said. "Hell, we've been in danger every day for the last couple of years. This'll be different, but at least we'll be *doing* something. . . ." He turned away from the CCs and addressed the rest of the group. "I think it's a good plan, and I'd like to be a part of it. But if you want to keep on going, I'll yield to the majority."

"I say we fight," Kirk responded, shaking a fist in the air.

"I just want to stay with you, Dad," said Ryan.

"And I feel the same way," Karen added, draping her arm around Ryan's shoulders.

"Even if I wasn't already outvoted," said Jerry, "I'd want to help. But I have more than myself to think about." He turned to Suzie. "I won't leave you and Jacob. We can strike out on our own—"

"No." Suzie spoke quietly but firmly as she clutched her son to her breast. "You go and help these people. I know that's what you really want, and they need you, too. We'll find a place to stay and wait for you until it's over."

"I love you," Jerry said softly, putting his arms around his wife and child. "And I won't let you down." Then he turned toward Tony and Richard and said, "It looks like we're all in this together. So what do we do next?"

17

March 26, 2037

"It'll be another week or two before we're sure," said General Garrison. "But it looks more and more all the time like the xenoborgs are playing right into our hands."

The general moved back to his seat at the front of the auditorium, a signal that the formal part of the briefing was over. Traynor stood and walked to the microphone. "Questions and comments," he announced. "One at a time, please!" he added as twenty cybernetic hands went into the air and a dozen voices all spoke out at the same time.

Ever since the formulation of Operation Manpower, practically all CC briefings had been conducted en masse because every team operating out of the Manitowoc base was working toward the same objective. From the standpoint of those in charge, it was more efficient to impart information to large groups instead of addressing only four, six, or eight CCs at one time. However, the mass meetings did tend to make the customary question-and-answer period more than a little chaotic.

Cris, Maura, Tony, and Richard sat quietly, willing to bide their time and see whether their own questions would be asked by another of the three hundred Cyborg Commandos in the auditorium.

Traynor acknowledged an eager CC in the front row — probably a new recruit, he thought, who wants to impress everyone else with his wisdom and insight. Well, let's see. . . .

"It's good news, sir, but how can we be sure the xenoborgs don't have something else in mind?"

"We can't," answered Traynor, hoping he didn't sound as exasperated as he felt. "Since we can't read their minds and will probably never be able to, all we can do is draw conclusions based on observation and conjecture. We're fighting an enemy that doesn't act like we do and doesn't think like we do. Be assured that the people who assess information and make judgments on it are not born optimists — in fact, they're quite the opposite. So if they say that this xenoborg migration, or whatever it is, can be turned to our advantage, then I'm inclined to believe them." The CC in the front row took his seat silently and, Traynor thought, a little sheepishly.

"I can see how this might cause us to change

our plans," said another CC when Traynor nodded in his direction. "But how will they change, and how much?"

"We don't know right now," said Traynor. "We need another week or two, like the general said, to ascertain the scope and speed of this apparent withdrawal. If every xenoborg in the upper Midwest goes crawling back to Milwaukee, then Operation Manpower has a much greater chance of succeeding because, obviously, we'll have a lot less territory to cover. But if what we're observing is only a partial migration, then the plan won't change in any general way, but we may have to reallocate some of the teams.

"In any event, getting down to detail like that right now would be counterproductive, because we have no way of knowing what the situation will be like when we're in a position to start moving against the recharging sites. All of you will be advised immediately if and when your particular duties have to be changed. In the meantime, the standing orders are still in effect. We still need more people and materials. In that respect, the plan hasn't changed at all."

The questions and answers went on for another half hour. Cris kept half an ear on the proceedings, perking up when a change in Traynor's tone of voice foretold some new and useful bit of information. Most of the time he let his mind wander back over what the general had said earlier, trying to fit it all together into a conclusion of his own.

Nearly every CC team in Manitowoc's area of responsibility had experienced the same frustration and confusion as Cris's team when it came to flushing out and finishing off small groups of xenoborgs. As recently as ten days ago, it was a rare occurrence indeed when a team of CCs on patrol did not locate at least one group of scavenging xenoborgs in a single day of scouting around. But now the pendulum had swung the other way; finding a small group of monsters was the exception rather than the rule.

In the last three or four days, several teams had witnessed incidents similar to what Cris and his comrades had seen on the highway — caravans containing anywhere from ten to fifty monsters proceeding slowly but persistently on a beeline for the Milwaukee metropolitan area. Reports from as far away as Minnesota and Iowa described long lines of xenoborgs heading in that direction.

They paused or veered from their course only to eat, and even when they did that they seemed to be mechanical about it — consuming enough to keep themselves nourished but not going about it with their characteristic viciousness. They found food, not caring if it was animal or vegetable, they ingested it, they re-formed into a long line, and they moved on. Cris's impression of the group he and his team had seen was supported by the observations of other CCs: the xenoborgs were intent on getting to their destination, and nothing else mattered. . . .

Cris's musing was interrupted as Tony, who had been seated beside him, got to his feet, timing his move so that he would be intercepted by Traynor's sweeping gaze.

"If we know where these caravans are and where they're headed," he began, "then why don't we send up some planes and missiles and blast 'em?" Cris thought he saw the general flinch as the man realized who the questioner was, and he was glad for Tony's sake that this was not a small-group briefing — or his friend would probably have been the object of General Garrison's scorn once again.

"We considered that — briefly," said Traynor. "But we don't necessarily want to discourage them from doing what they're doing. They're not aggressive, they're not causing a great deal of new destruction, and they're not going out of their way to kill human beings. So we're not inclined to waste firepower and tear up a whole lot of landscape and run the risk of getting them riled up again."

"Live and let live, huh?" Tony shot out before Traynor could acknowledge another questioner. This time Cris winced inside as the general shot to his feet.

"No!" General Garrison boomed. "The only way we can win this war is to conserve our resources and use them in ways that will do the most good.

We're not 'letting them live,' we're waiting for the right opportunity to take out as many as we can all at once. And what they're doing right now, if we leave them alone and allow them to finish doing it, is going to make our job that much easier. If the way to win this war was an all-out frontal attack, we would have sent all of you into Milwaukee a long time ago. Would you like to volunteer to lead that mission, sergeant?"

"No, sir," said Tony, just loud enough to be heard. Then he muttered to Cris as he sank back into his seat. "Why do I seem to get his dander up every time I ask a question?"

Cris stifled the urge to laugh, and was glad he did when he realized Tony wasn't trying to be funny. "I don't think it has anything to do with you," Cris ventured kindly. "I think it's just that you seem to ask questions that hit a nerve with him. I get the sense that he really *does* want to send a bunch of us over the hill to start shooting away. But at the same time, he knows that would be suicidal. He feels helpless, and he gets even more frustrated whenever somebody else starts talking about 'blasting 'em.' I could be wrong, but I think the two of you have a lot in common."

"I agree," said Tony.

"You do?"

"Yeah. With the part about how you could be wrong. Me and Garrison have about as much in common as a—" Tony wasn't able to finish that thought. A familiar voice from the front of the room stopped him.

"Sergeant S-24, since you seem to think that whatever you have to say to your partner is more important than listening to what's being said up here, how about sharing your brilliant observations with the rest of us?"

Very few of the CCs attending the briefing would ever forget — or be able to remember without laughing — what happened next. Sergeant S-24 stood up, cleared his throat, and answered the general's question by saying, "I was saying I didn't think you and I have much in common, sir."

Cris and Tony couldn't hear any response from the general, although they could hardly miss the way his face turned a brilliant shade of red. Later they found out from someone seated in the front row that the general did say something. With the expletives deleted, it boiled down to "One of the few things I have to be thankful for these days!"

* * *

When the big briefing ended and the four of them were alone, Cris kicked off the conversation with his best impersonation of Traynor. "Questions and comments — one at a time, please."

Tony turned his head quickly from side to side, looking over each shoulder. "What do you mean, 'No'?" Maura asked.

"I wasn't saying no," Tony answered. "Just trying to see if the general was anywhere in the vicinity before I opened my mouth again."

Richard got the discussion back on track by repeating a theory that had been brought up during the briefing. "A withdrawal — if that's what this is — is not necessarily a retreat," he said. "I sure hope they aren't reading this the wrong way."

"Me too," said Cris, inwardly pleased to hear that Richard wasn't blindly accepting the interpretation the experts had placed on the xenoborg migration. "I'd like to believe that they're pulling back with the intention of giving up, but I'm not convinced."

"Nobody's convinced yet," said Maura, taking the role of devil's advocate even though she shared Cris's sentiments. "Maybe the point of all this will become clear in the next couple of weeks. For now, we just have to keep doing our jobs."

"Nobody's arguing with that," said Tony. "And even if they want to retreat and leave the planet, how are they going to get away? Do you suppose we're going to switch off the defense system and let them bring down transport vessels because we *think* they're going to use them to leave?"

That was a good point, Cris told himself. Mankind had followed the success of Operation Chase Into Space, in which all of the xenoborgs' original transport vessels — called "teleborgs" — had been destroyed, with the launching of a group of surveillance satellites designed to prevent any more teleborgs from entering the atmosphere. The defense network had done its job, obliterating the few foreign bodies that had attempted to approach the planet in the last several months. But the same shield that had kept the xenoborgs from adding to their forces would also prevent them from escaping, if that was what they intended to do — unless mankind took the life-or-death gamble of shutting down the satellites and letting teleborgs land on the planet once again. He couldn't imagine any of the military planners being so optimistic that they would suggest that course of action.

"So what we'll be faced with, in the best case," Cris said, "is a few thousand xenoborgs clustered in one area with no place to go."

"A standoff," said Richard. "They keep places like Milwaukee and Kansas City, and we get to keep everything in between."

"Wrong," Tony cut in emphatically. "As long as I live and breathe, so to speak, I'm not going to put up with any deal like that. Nothing on this planet belongs to them, and they don't belong here. Either they leave or they die — it's as simple as that."

"I feel the same way," Richard responded, anxious to correct Tony's mistaken impression. "I don't want a standoff — I don't want a compromise either. I'm saying that maybe that's what *they're* going for."

"Could be," said Maura. "But again, that's something we can't speculate on until we learn more about what's happening right now."

"And we're not going to get more information by sitting here and exercising our voice simulators," said Cris. "I say we head back to the recruiting station and keep on doing what they're paying us for."

"Some pay," Tony grumbled facetiously. "A fresh dose of electricity every couple of days and a blistering lecture from General Garrison every time I open my mouth."

"So what are you complaining about?" asked Cris with a chuckle. "That's more than I get, and I'm the boss!"

18

April 9, 2037

A group of about twenty people were gathered around the dining-room table at the Larson residence. Another fifteen were in the kitchen, and twenty more were busy working on the floor in the living room. Ryan and several other children were in constant motion back and forth between the three groups, carefully ferrying a limited supply of scissors, needles, and other pieces of equipment from those who had finished with them to those who needed them.

By late afternoon the job was done. "That sews this one up," Dan quipped, causing Karen and a couple of others within hearing to chuckle.

"With a net gain of one," Karen said with a smirk, getting up off the living-room floor where she had been hard at work helping the others in the group stitch rubber lining around the edge of a large, sturdy net.

She stood, bent over, and rolled the finished product into a neat, compact bundle — one that could easily be carried by a member of Operation Manpower.

"How many does that make now?" a squat, bald-headed man asked as he stood up and brushed off his pants.

"That's our fourth net, to go along with four tarpaulins — all the equipment we were given to prepare, and all we should need for a group this size," Dan said.

"When do we get our escort?" a rather plump middle-aged woman asked.

"We were told to expect Sergeant T-56 sometime tomorrow morning. Then we start heading south, getting into position. Until then, I guess we can just relax," Karen said tiredly but cheerfully. She was feeling a sense of renewed hope, bred from the activity geared toward fighting the evil that had ripped her world to shreds. Finally, she thought, mankind was on the verge of making a unified stand against the alien intruders.

And there was another reason why Karen Sullivan was feeling more alive and happier these days.

"So, do you intend to do this 'relaxing' alone? Or would you like some company?" Dan interrupted her thoughts.

"What do you have in mind?" Karen teased, knowing full well the answer to that question before she voiced it.

* * *

When they had first discussed their feelings forthrightly a little less than two weeks earlier, after arriving at the Larson homestead, both Karen and Dan had acknowledged that they had grown to care very deeply for each other. Even so, Dan was concerned that his affection for Karen was an act of disloyalty to his late wife. "She hasn't been dead that long, and, to be honest with you, I still love her and miss her," Dan had told Karen.

"I wouldn't want you to ever stop loving or missing her. What you and Sharon had was obviously very special, and I envy you that," Karen had said very seriously. "But, Dan, Sharon *is* gone. And we have to go on living. If we're lucky enough to have found love in the midst of this insanity, I think we should enjoy it for all it's worth!"

Dan hadn't said anything after that. He had just held Karen until both of them fell asleep, sitting up beside each other on the living-room couch. The next day Dan had gone for a walk — alone. And when he came back he had quietly taken his place beside Karen and had worked on preparing one of the nets in silence.

After all of the work for that day was finished

and Ryan had been put to bed, he sought her out again. He found her sitting on the railing of the porch that ran along the front of the Larson home. She looked up and smiled warmly, expectantly, at him as he approached.

"Karen . . ." he began, not quite knowing where he'd find the words. And then, simply, and with more love and passion than he had thought he would ever feel again, he said, "I want you."

He offered her his hand, and Karen took it without hesitation. For what seemed like an eternity, the two stood face to face, savoring the realization that, from now on, for as long as they both lived, neither of them would have to face another day — or night — alone.

And that night, their memories of all of the previous evenings of fear and sadness were briefly submerged. They forgot about the world around them and gave themselves to each other.

They made love in the hayloft of the rundown barn on the Larson farm. There were no silk sheets, no bottles of champagne chilling in crystal ice buckets. But thoughts like those were far from their minds.

"I never thought I'd say this to another woman, but . . . I love you, Karen. It's a different love than I felt for . . . her . . . but it's no less intense."

"I love you, too," Karen answered. . . .

When the first rays of sunlight poked through the same cracks where moonlight had streamed hours earlier, they fell upon two people who were wide awake and serenely happy. They had exchanged vows without speaking a word, and each knew the other would honor the lifelong commitment.

* * *

The following days passed quickly, and the population of the homestead grew. After Dan, Karen, and the others had agreed to take part in Operation Manpower, Dan had suggested to their CC "recruiters" that the Larsons might be willing to allow the use of their home as a gathering place for other participants.

Andrew didn't bat an eye when the carload of people returned to the house and asked if they could stay a while longer. And he positively beamed when Dan hesitantly added that they could expect other guests to be trickling in for the next couple of weeks. "Somethin's goin' on, ain't it?" he asked with a twinkle in his eye. Dan nodded to that, and then explained to the Larsons everything he had been told about Operation Manpower.

The old man smacked his fist into his palm repeatedly as Dan went through the details. "So they finally thought o' somethin', eh?" he said when Dan had finished. The words had come out in a sarcastic tone, but the pride behind them was evident in his voice as well. "What do we do first?"

Dan then went on to recite what he had been told about how to prepare the gear they would need.

"A group of soldiers will be along in the next day or so to drop off some netting and maybe also some large tarpaulins. Those are what we'll use to either pull the things out of the water or cover them so they can't get any sunlight. But we can't use them the way they are — anybody who touches one of the things, or anything they come in contact with, without being insulated will get electrocuted."

"So we get us some rubber boots and rubber gloves," said Andrew, sitting back as though he had just solved all the world's problems.

"As many as we can find, yes," said Dan. "But there won't be enough to go around, so what we have to do is take strips of rubber or soft plastic and attach them to the edges of the nets and tarps. That way everyone will be protected from the electricity, not just the ones who are lucky enough to have boots and gloves."

"Hmmph. Haven't missed a trick, have they?" said Andrew.

"I sure hope not," Dan answered. "I sure hope not. . . ."

* * *

As promised, Sergeant T-56 arrived at the home early on the morning of April 10. Andrew

Larson was more than a little tickled when he heard the cyborg say to the assembled group, "Call me Andy."

"How 'bout that!" the old man crowed, moving forward to offer his hand. "I'm Andy, too — Andrew Larson, the owner o' this place."

"My full name is Andrew Ambach," said the CC, returning the formality, "and I'm very glad to meet you."

"Ambach . . ." said the man thoughtfully. "Any relation to old Jeff Ambach, the guy who used t' deliver the mail around here?"

"I don't think so," answered the cyborg politely. "Is there anything I can do for you before we get going?" he added in an effort to get the proceedings back on track.

"I s'pose not," said Andrew after a moment. Then a thought struck him. "Say, you wouldn't have time to blast me a few holes for fenceposts, would you?"

"I'll tell you what, Mr. Larson — Andrew," the young man replied. "When we get done with what we have to do, I'll try to have someone stop back and do exactly that."

"No hurry," said the old man. "I got time," he added wistfully.

"We have to be on our way," Dan said, stepping up to face the old man. "We'll be back as soon as we can. In the meantime—"

"Don't worry about a thing," Andrew broke in.

"We can take care o' things around here," he went on, his spirits lifted again. "Tell y' what — first chance y' get to beat up on one o' those monsters, give it a good shot for me."

Ten minutes later, after a final round of good-byes between those who were leaving and those who were staying behind, Sergeant T-56 led forty people out the front door of the Larson home and down the narrow road leading to the highway.

Throughout the midwestern United States and all around the world, tens of thousands of other groups were doing the same thing.

Operation Manpower was under way.

19

April 10, 2037

"Are you sure?" asked Cris, even though he knew what the answer would be.

"No. The word doesn't apply in the pure sense," said Traynor. "But we're as sure as we can be, if you can accept that slight qualification. We haven't seen any, so we can be *pretty* sure there aren't any out there to be seen."

Almost five full days had elapsed since any Cyborg Commando team in the upper Midwest had reported any xenoborg movement or activity. It seemed as though all the monsters that once had roamed within a radius of several hundred miles around Manitowoc were now congregated in Milwaukee.

The exodus had been awesome in its scope. From as far west as the eastern Dakotas and as far south as Kentucky, the monsters had simply dropped what they were doing, formed into caravans, and headed on an unwavering course for what was left of the once-proud city on the shore of Lake Michigan. Now, apparently, they all had arrived at their common destination . . . and the next move was up to mankind.

The prevailing opinion among the strategists had not changed. This migration, or retreat, or whatever it was, would help Operation Manpower to succeed. Instead of having to patrol hundreds of thousands of square miles of terrain, the netting teams and the CCs backing them up would only have to concern themselves with a much smaller area — the city of Milwaukee and its immediate environs.

Of course, it wasn't that simple. The military experts had also dutifully pointed out that although the netting teams would have to cover a relatively small number of recharging sites, all of those locations would be inside occupied territory. Every human being and every Cyborg Commando committed to the plan would be putting his or her life at risk for not just a few minutes at a time, but for every minute of every day as long as they remained inside the perimeter of the territory controlled by the xenoborgs.

"So what do we do now?" asked Tony. "Is it time to move into position?"

"Yes," said Traynor. "At this moment, the rest of

the CCs and regular soldiers attached to this base are getting their general orders. They have about a day to get into the field, rendezvous with their attack groups, and form into a loose ring around the greater Milwaukee area. Operation Manpower will get under way at 1900 hours tomorrow."

Cris felt the excitement well up inside him, and when Maura reached out and took his hand he thought he could feel her eager apprehension in the way she squeezed his fingers. The battle that would decide the fate of the planet, one way or the other, was finally about to begin.

"But why are we here instead of in the general briefing?" Richard asked. Cris chided himself silently for getting caught up in his thoughts — that was a question, he thought, that should have occurred to him.

"You folks have been given something special to do before joining in the general assault," said Traynor. "Reconnaissance."

"But we know where all the xenoborgs are," said Cris. "What's the point of a scouting mission?"

"Until we know *exactly* where they are," Traynor explained, "we can't establish a firm perimeter. Have the monsters pulled back all the way into the urban area, or are they scattered through the outskirts of the city? Will our initial resistance be sporadic or concentrated? Have the xenoborgs taken a defensive posture, expecting us to come after them, or are they just milling around?

"Those are questions we can't answer without reconnaissance. You are one of six teams we're sending out to determine the precise outer boundary of the occupied area, and to find out exactly what we'll be up against when we try to penetrate or push back that boundary."

"Okay," said Cris, his tone carrying a combination of determination and eager anxiety. "Exactly what do you want us to do?"

* * *

"This is nice," said Tony to no one in particular. "A little weird, but nice."

Cris and his team were moving southward cautiously because, as Traynor had driven home to them, they couldn't be *absolutely* sure there were no xenoborgs lurking between Manitowoc and Milwaukee. But with almost every step they took, it became harder and harder to stay in an on-the-lookout frame of mind. The day was warm and sunny, and except for occasional evidence of the xenoborgs' former presence — crumpled underbrush, abandoned and dilapidated buildings — rural southeastern Wisconsin seemed as pristine and beautiful as it had been in the days before the invasion.

"Spooky," suggested Maura. "Too good to be true."

"Yeah," Cris muttered absently.

"Aw, let's savor the moment," Tony said in a cavalier tone. "I know as well as you do that the peace and quiet isn't gonna last. So why not enjoy it while we can?"

His question went unanswered as all four of the CCs continued to wind their way south. They had been made responsible for reconnaissance on the extreme northern rim, and were moving on a course that kept them within two to three miles of Lake Michigan at all times. Their orders were straightforward: proceed south until they saw a concentration of xenoborgs or until they reached the edge of the Milwaukee metropolitan area. If they got that far south and still had not seen any monsters, then they could be sure that, at least in their sector, the xenoborgs had not remained in or ventured into the outlying areas.

That little piece of information, coupled with similar reports from the other reconnaissance teams moving toward the city from the west and south, would tell the strategists exactly how far the assault teams could advance before Operation Manpower would actually begin. If the netting squads set up in too loose a perimeter, they would waste time and effort trying to set their traps in bodies of water that were outside the monsters' area of occupation. If they came in too close before starting to search for recharging sites, some of them might be detected, overrun, and cut off by a sudden counterattack.

Timing, positioning, and stealth were of utmost importance; after the assault teams formed a ring around the city, the ring had to remain unbroken. If it was breached, the humans and CCs would lose the advantage of keeping all the xenoborgs corraled within their perimeter — and losing that advantage could be the difference between victory and defeat.

* * *

"We're getting close," said Cris, lowering his voice to a whisper for the first time since their excursion had begun. "Step lightly." It was just after 1800, with the assault teams scheduled to start moving up to their initial positions in less than an hour, and Cris estimated that he and his team were about five miles north of the line separating the metropolitan area from the northern suburbs. So far they had not seen or heard any unusual or threatening activity — but now, with every step they took, the likelihood of running into the enemy was measurably greater.

The terrain rose in a gradual incline from where they were; roughly three miles away on the horizon was the top of a ridge. At their current pace, they would be at that location in about fifteen minutes, and from that vantage point they would be able to see at least a couple of miles farther south — right up to the fringe of the city.

"It won't be long now," said Tony, his anxiety showing in his voice.

"We'll be home free before you know it," Cris said lightly, hoping to ease the tension. "All we have to do is make it to the top of this ridge. Let's fan out, and keep an eye on the flanks too," he added.

They advanced up the incline four abreast, spaced about fifty yards apart. Cris, in one of the middle positions between Richard and Maura, kept flicking his gaze back and forth from east to west. He wasn't as worried about what might be waiting to the south as he was about what might be lurking to the sides. If they had unknowingly penetrated beyond the edge of the xenoborgs' occupied territory, they could be surrounded and cut off before they could do anything about it. He didn't want get caught behind enemy lines, to have to fight his way back to safety.

The next few minutes were as uneventful as the last several hours had been: no unusual sights, no unusual sounds. When they were within two hundred feet of the top of the ridge, Cris extended his arms, the palms of his hands facing the ground, and signaled for everyone to get down. To keep from being sighted by any lookouts scanning the ridge from the other side, they would finish the journey by crawling up the slope, pulling themselves along with knees and elbows.

With precision that came from experience, all

four of them reached the top of the ridge simultaneously. Each of them spent the next two seconds assessing the vista that had just come into view before them. And that was where the similarity ended.

Richard buried his face in his hands and rubbed at his eye sockets, as though trying to erase the image they had just taken in.

Tony, never at a loss for words, began saying "Damn!" over and over as he stared at the scene.

Maura, after weathering the initial shock, turned toward Cris to see his reaction.

Cris didn't move or speak, but his mind was racing. What should they do? What *could* they do? How could they fight this?

Strung out before him at a distance of about a mile, spread in a gentle arc that extended as far as he could see to the east and the west, was a twitching, pulsating wall of creatures, each of which was facing away from the city . . . toward the general direction where Cris and his comrades were hiding. It contained xenoborgs — more monsters than he could count, more aliens than he could conceive of being in one place at one time. It also contained a much greater number of other creatures, and the longer he looked at them, the more unbelieving and more terrified he became.

They looked like cockroaches, ants, beetles . . . more different types of insects than he could identify. But they couldn't be Earth insects — they were huge! Although not nearly as large as the xenoborgs, they were still dozens or hundreds of times wider, taller, and longer . . . and stronger, he supposed . . . than ordinary bugs. They outnumbered the xenoborgs at least ten to one, from what he could see. They filled all the gaps in the line between one alien monster and the next, each one a link in a solid chain.

For the longest thirty seconds in his life, Cris peered out at the impossible sight. Then, just as he had succeeded in convincing himself that it *wasn't* impossible, just as he was on the verge of coming to his senses and deciding what to do, he saw and heard something that made him scream with terror inside.

All of a sudden, in mindless and mechanical unison, every creature in the line began to move slowly forward, outward. And as the wall moved, it trampled and tore up whatever was in the way. Xenoborg weapons flashed and exploded all along the line, demolishing buildings, cutting down trees, reducing every sizable obstacle to rubble or flaming debris.

The enemy was on the march. And in its wake, it was leaving nothing standing. Nothing alive. . . .

20

April 10-11, 2037

In a thirty-minute span of time between 1810 and 1840 hours, each of the six reconnaissance teams reported back to the Manitowoc base. To no one's surprise, the radio messages came in right on schedule. But to the utter astonishment of the people who received the computer-encoded transmissions, every one of them said essentially the same thing:

"Pull back! Take cover! Xenoborgs and giant insects are moving this way — and destroying everything in sight!"

That was exactly the message Cris had sent at about 1820 hours. When he got his wits about him again after watching long enough to get an unmistakable impression of what was happening — long enough to make him believe the scene before his eyes — he ordered Tony, Maura, and Richard to follow him, and all four of them headed north at top speed. When they reached the top of another ridge about a mile from their previous position, Cris stopped and turned on his transmitter to convey what little information he had to offer . . . just a couple of facts, but in themselves enough to spell possible doom for Operation Manpower.

To augment his "verbal" report — which was actually more a transmission of thoughts than of actual words — Cris patched in the video recorder that was contained within his internal computer and sent along electronic pulses that could be decoded into actual images. Roughly ten minutes after he and his team had abandoned their observation post, technicians and planners at the Manitowoc base were seeing exactly what Lieutenant P-17 had seen.

But would they perceive it the same way? Would they feel terror and panic gripping their hearts as he had? Would they *know* what they were seeing — and more importantly, would they know what to do about it?

As he asked himself those last two questions, Cris had to answer each of them in the negative. He was positive that no one had anticipated this possibility; the setup of the assault teams had been predicated on the supposedly safe assumption that the xenoborgs were going to stay put, and so the humans and CCs would be able to go in after them, drawing the ring of "fishing" squads tighter and tighter until they squeezed the monsters to death.

All that was out the window now, or so it seemed. Everyone would have to pull back and fan out. Instead of only having to patrol and control the relatively few bodies of water in the immediate area of Milwaukee, they would now have to revert to the original plan and try to stake out the innumerable lakes, rivers, streams, and ponds in all of Wisconsin, Minnesota, Iowa, and northern Illinois.

That alone would be hard enough to accomplish, but that wasn't even the worst problem the human race was facing now. While the "fishermen" set up outposts and waited, not so patiently, to see if the xenoborgs would use this place, or that, as a recharging site, the monsters and their hideous insect allies would be turning every square foot of ground they passed over into charred, broken, lifeless terrain. Even if Operation Manpower eventually succeeded in its original intent, what sort of a world would be left? What would the people who had risked their lives have as a reward for their efforts? Much of the world would be a wasteland, devastated as thoroughly as if it had been hit by nuclear weapons. How could man claim victory if the world he fought to save had been killed in the process?

"Cris?"

Maura's gentle voice snapped him out of his

thoughts, but not out of his mood. He looked at her, and for the umpteenth time wished he had a *real* face, and *real* eyes, so that she could read in his gaze and his expression the feelings he didn't want to verbalize.

"I'm okay," he said, trying to sound like he meant it.

"If you are, then you're the only one," said Tony sincerely.

"Now you have some idea what Maura and I saw in the woods that night," Cris said to Tony and Richard.

"I think 'some idea' is putting it mildly," Richard observed. "God, they weren't leaving *anything* standing. . . ."

"It was the same way in the woods," said Maura. "Only then, it was just six xenoborgs. Now, for all we know, there are thousands of xenoborgs and God knows how many of those other . . . things . . . all doing it at once."

"Those 'things' look pretty much like plain old insects," said Tony. "But how did they get so big and strong?"

"A couple of reasons I can think of," Cris responded. He was quietly pleased with the turn the conversation had taken; as long as they talked objectively and clinically, trying to understand what they had seen, and stayed away from how they felt about it, he would be able to keep his emotions under control until they subsided. And he had a hunch the others were thinking, at least subconsciously, the same way.

"Maybe the xenoborgs have some way of breeding insects to make them larger and stronger," he continued. "Maybe that's what they've been doing while they were holed up in all of their occupied cities for all these months. Maybe this has been part of their strategy all along."

"A lot of maybes all strung together," said Tony, "but maybe you have something there. What's your other theory?"

"The other possibility is that they haven't been planning this for a long time, and they've just recently come up with a way to grow giant insects or create mutations to help them carry out a plan they've just developed."

"And that plan is . . . ?" prompted Richard, asking Cris the question in a tone that indicated he already knew the answer.

"Twentieth-century historians had a term for it: scorched earth. In other words, if they can't have the planet, they want to make sure there's nothing left of it for us, either. Consider what's happened in the last couple of years. They came down and just about knocked us out — but they didn't get the job done. We fought back and accomplished some things I'm sure they didn't think we were capable of. Recently — until a few minutes ago, at least — we've been at a standoff. They've grabbed and held a few dozen major cities, but we again have control over more than ninety percent of the world's land area. They must have come to realize that they couldn't hold the cities forever, that they were fighting a losing battle. So instead of sitting tight, they're moving out. Maybe we'll kill them all once they spread out and we can take them on in small-group encounters. But by then—"

"Helluva speech, pal," said Tony. Cris, in retrospect, was grateful for the interruption; he had been on the verge of getting into a subject area he didn't really want to talk about. "But I think you're giving these bastards too much credit. They can't 'realize' what they're doing, or they wouldn't be doing it. If they keep on smashing and burning until there's nothing left, then they're as good as dead, too — if not dead already. Maybe if we had a way of getting that across to them, we could get them to stop."

"Oh, good," said Maura, exaggerating the second word. "Now, instead of 'blasting 'em,' he wants to *reason* with them! My, haven't we come a long way?"

"That's not what I—" Tony began in an irritated tone, then sputtered as he realized she was joking. "Oh, hell! I think I'd rather be yelled at by that old bat General Garrison. At least when he says something to me, there's no mistake about what he means."

Except for a couple of chuckles from Cris and Richard, no one said anything after that for a few seconds. Then, suddenly, Cris's hand darted up to the side of his head. "Uh, oh," he muttered.

"What is it?" asked Maura quickly.

"The base just tried to send us a message."

"Tried?"

"Yeah, but I didn't catch all of it right away, and they had to repeat the first few bits. My transmitter's been on ever since I made my report," he added sheepishly.

"You mean they've been listening to . . . ?" Tony dropped his head into his hands and let the rest of the question trail off, so Maura finished it for him.

"Yes, Tony. Everything we've said." She giggled, Cris and Richard had another chuckle, and Tony just let out a soft moan.

* * *

The message, a direct communication from Traynor, concerned their new orders and gave them an update on the state of affairs. The reconnaissance reports had been received in time; new instructions had been relayed to the CCs and troops who were overseeing and administering the assault teams, and everyone had settled into positions where they would be in no immediate danger from the advancing horde. The assumption all four of them had instinctively made was correct: the line of xenoborgs and insects was radiating outward from Milwaukee to the north, west, and south. Fortunately, the creatures seemed to be moving extremely slowly, averaging considerably less than a mile an hour.

Cris's team and the other five reconnaissance squads were assigned to keep falling back slowly: find a good vantage point, hold that position until the creatures came into view once again, make a report, and then withdraw another mile or so and repeat the process. Under no circumstances were they to take offensive action or otherwise reveal their presence to the enemy.

The part of the communication that Traynor had to repeat ended with two remarks that were neither informational nor instructional. First, "Thanks for the input," and then, "The general sends his regards." When Cris conveyed those two sentences to the rest of the group, Tony became even more theatrical than before.

"Oh, woe is me!" he said. "I may as well go try to negotiate with those bugs. I'd stand a better chance with them than I would with you know who."

"Unless you really mean that," said Maura, "I think we'd all better prepare to get a move on." She cocked her thumb toward the southern sky, where the bright flashes of laser bursts and the soft glow of burning wreckage had started to become visible against the darkening sky. The monsters were about to come over the top of the ridge.

"Shouldn't we wait until we actually see them?"

Richard asked "Isn't that what the orders specified?"

"We're about a mile away from the edge of that rise," said Cris. "A wayward laser beam can cover that distance in less time than—"

"Say no more," Richard broke in, embarrassed but not intimidated.

"Don't feel too bad," Tony whispered to Richard as the four of them headed north. "I was just about to ask the same question."

* * *

At daybreak the next morning, Cris got another direct communication from Traynor. It wasn't good news, but at least it wasn't more of the other kind.

"I fed your theories to the big thinkers," the message began, "and they liked number two. If the big insects had existed for any length of time, we would have found out about them before now. Our guess is that they were grown, or mutated by means of radiation, in the last two weeks or less. That means this plan of theirs hasn't been long in the making — it was put together hastily, out of desperation, and not in anticipation of what we've been planning. Every plan has a weak spot, and plans that are formed in a hurry have more weaknesses than others.

"We'll find the weak spots, Cris. All we need is time."

Right, Cris thought. Time. . . . And with every little slice of time that passes, another large chunk of this planet gets broken, trampled, and incinerated. Take your time, Traynor — just don't take too much more.

"A solenoid for your thoughts," said Maura, dropping prone next to where Cris was lying on his stomach surveying the valley they had crossed just before taking up this surveillance position.

"I can't get my mind off Traynor's last sentence. He says they need time, and meanwhile . . ."

"I know what you're saying. But we have to give them a chance to figure something out, and we have to hope that they'll do just that. There's not much else we can do right now except wait and hope."

"Yeah. I just wish we had less time to wait and more to hope for."

A few minutes later, Cris's wish came true.

Because of the terrain in this area, the CCs could establish and maintain visual contact with the line of creatures without putting themselves in danger. They were flattened out on the northern side of an outcropping of rock, and by peering through crevices in the surface they could scan the full width of the steep-walled valley they had come across. It was a carpet of green, bright even in the diffused light of early morning — mostly grassland dotted by a few solitary trees. For several yards on either side of a placid stream that bisected the depression, the vegetation was tall and thick, already benefitting this early in the growing season from being closer to the life-giving water.

When the creatures moved into the valley, Cris and his comrades stayed where they were. The xenoborgs with lasers and projectile weapons were keeping them aimed parallel to the down-sloping terrain, so there was virtually no chance that a wild shot would come anywhere near the rocks that crested the other side of the depression.

This time, because he knew what to expect, Cris found it somewhat easier to watch the destruction taking place. Instead of horrifying, it was "merely" disgusting; instead of being shocked, he found himself filling with rage. This *had* to stop, he thought. . . .

And then it did.

When the line was about fifty yards from the stream, the leader-type xenoborgs abruptly stopped moving forward and stopped using their weapons. That must have been a signal to the other xenoborgs and all the insects, because within seconds every other creature in the onslaught was also stationary.

Although this was just as unexpected as what he had seen at sunset the night before, this time Cris had no trouble believing what he was seeing — because he *wanted* to believe it. Even as he savored the happy excitement welling up inside him, he fought to suppress it; before he celebrated *what* was happening, he wanted to figure out *why*. He knew he should report the information quickly, but he waited in hopes of finding out more.

They're paralyzed, he thought, then instantly dismissed that idea. Mandibles and pincers still clicked and twitched, tentacles and antennae still waved and wriggled. They were quite alive and apparently capable of movement, only all of a sudden they weren't going anywhere.

No . . . that wasn't completely true. As Cris watched what happened next, he stopped trying to figure out what was going on. He didn't have to do that — he *knew*.

Several of the ordinary, weaponless xenoborgs left their places in the line, each moving toward the nearest leader-type. They reached inside the leaders' bodies and extracted as many powwers as they could carry. Then they shuffled down to the stream, gently deposited the silver objects in the water, and went back for more.

"Wow!" said Tony under his breath.

"Just watch!" Cris hissed, keeping his gaze fixed on what was in front of him. "Try not to miss a thing."

Half an hour later, when the extraction process was apparently complete, all of the normal xenoborgs took their places in the line once again. And then every creature in the entire ghastly, unearthly procession stayed right where it was.

After watching the immobile, silent menagerie

for a few more minutes, Cris motioned for the others to gather around him. Before he could prompt anyone for an opinion, Maura spoke up, her voice conveying a strange mixture of seriousness and exhilaration.

"I have a feeling," she said, emphasizing the word to make sure he understood, "that they aren't going anywhere for quite a while."

Cris reached out and put his hand on her shoulder. "And I have a hunch," he said, imitating her tone of voice, "that we just found the weak spot."

21

April 11, 2037

For his next report to the Manitowoc base, Cris was determined not to repeat the style of the disjointed, frantic message he had sent less than twelve hours earlier. He concentrated on staying cool and dispassionate.

And he succeeded . . . for the first ten words or so.

"The enemy has stopped," he began. "They're just on the other side of a stream and . . . and Maura says they're not going anywhere for a while! They dumped their powwers in the water, and now they're waiting for them to recharge, so we should get in here—" He stopped, realizing he was getting out of control, switched off his transmitter, and tried to collect himself.

"Oh, hell," he muttered to cover his embarrassment, looking around at his teammates. "I'll just give 'em the video." He began transmitting again, this time instantaneously patching in the pictures his internal computer had stored. The images, which had already been translated from patterns of light and color into electrical impulses, could be sent back to the base in a small fraction of the time it had taken to record them. Three seconds later, he was done.

"Okay," he said. "Now we wait."

"Wait! Wait?!" Tony was incredulous. "Those bastards are just sitting there! We could slice 'em to pieces before—"

"We couldn't slice them *all* to pieces," Richard pointed out. "We'd be out of power long before that happened."

"Thank you, corporal," Cris said with exaggerated exasperation, "for saving me the trouble of having to point out that obvious fact to the overeager sergeant."

Tony bristled. "Jeez, have you been taking sarcasm lessons from the general?"

"And we don't want to get them mad, either," Maura contributed. "I'd rather have them right where they are instead of prompting them to go on the warpath again."

"But they're powwer-less," said Tony plaintively, still pressing the aggressive stance. "Now's our chance!"

"We can't be sure that the leaders, or at least

some of them, don't still have charged-up powwers inside," said Cris.

"I say we wait," he continued in his officer's voice. "It will take the people back at the base as long to review the video images as it took me to record them, and I think we can grant them some more time after that to figure out what to do.

"And let's not lose sight of the fact," he concluded, "that we're not four super-soldiers on our own, doing what *we* think is right, any more. There are thousands of people out here working with us. People who are willing, even eager, to help. People we *need*."

That, as Cris had intended, was the end of the discussion.

* * *

The sun was high in the sky and it was a beautiful day, which should have lifted Dan's spirits. He was physically comfortable, sitting with his back against a tree and his arm around Karen, but he was tense. This is what it must be like, he thought, to be on the front line just before the shooting starts.

Or was this the front line? He wasn't sure any more. . . .

Last evening, just as Dan and the group he was leading had moved into what they thought would be their final pre-assault position, they were accosted by a soldier weaving between the trees on a three-wheeled all-terrain vehicle. "You haven't heard!" shouted the man over the hum of the engine as he braked to a stop in front of Dan.

"Heard what?"

"New orders. Pull back ten miles. Everyone in this sector is too close to the xenoborgs. Someone else will be in touch tomorrow." Without waiting for questions or even an acknowledgment, he quickly pivoted the vehicle's front wheel and headed away to the east.

The group had spent the next five hours trekking back over ground they had just traversed. When Dan estimated they had gone the required distance, he instructed everyone to set up camp in the forest clearing they now occupied.

Half a day later, he was still waiting for "someone else" to show up, and getting more fidgety with every passing minute.

"Try to take it easy," said Karen, sensing his anxiety. "Worrying won't accomplish anything," she added, trying to be supportive.

"Neither will waiting," he shot back, more sharply than he meant it. "I just wish—"

"Dan! Dan!" Kirk was shouting his name and running toward him from one of the lookout posts that had been established. "A cyborg's coming this way — I think it's that Andy guy again."

Dan rose and trotted behind Kirk to the edge of the clearing, where they intercepted Sergeant T-56 as he was coming out of the trees. All Dan got out was "Hello" before he was interrupted.

"I have to hurry," said the CC briskly, "so listen closely. Plans have changed." As concisely as he could, Andy Ambach related what the leaders of Operation Manpower had learned, then finished by summarizing the new orders he was passing to every group he could locate.

"Advance toward Milwaukee during the day. If you find a potential recharging site, sink your nets and stake it out. If you find a site actually in use, get out your tarpaulins and try to throw a cover over as many powwers as possible. Fall back five or six miles during the late afternoon and evening, find another good spot to watch, and repeat the process until . . ." For the first time, the CC hesitated.

"Until we're done," Dan supplied, realizing the statement could be taken two ways.

"Right," the sergeant confirmed. "If you run across any other groups that haven't heard the new orders, tell them what I just told you. And . . . good luck." Without waiting for a response, the cyborg broke into a run and was out of sight in seconds.

"Giant insects, huh?" Kirk, who had overheard everything, made the comment with anticipation instead of dread. "I've always hated bugs," he added with a grin. "Maybe we can squash a few while we're at it."

"Get everybody together," Dan said to him, returning the smile. "We've got work to do!"

* * *

Later that day, the first time Dan Murphy saw one of the silver things known as powwers, he found it hard to believe that such an innocuous object could be at the root of all the tragedy and devastation that Earth had suffered. The *real* monsters are out there, he said to himself, his gaze sweeping across the horde of xenoborgs and insects resting — stationary but not dormant — about thirty yards south of the pond that he and the scouting party had just discovered.

But he knew what they had to do, and he was forming a plan of action even as the conflicting thoughts went through his mind. He turned and silently motioned for the rest of the scouts to follow him back to the main body of the group, which was holed up about a quarter-mile away.

After he had described the situation and issued instructions, four ten-member attack groups went forth, fanning out to take positions on three sides of the pond. The groups on the ends would be in the most danger because they would have to get closer to the enemy than any of the other attackers. Fortunately for them, they had tasks that would require them to be exposed and vulnerable for only about half a minute.

And fortunately for everyone, the pond was surrounded by three-foot-tall marsh grass that grew almost up to the shoreline, providing excellent cover. From that standpoint, forty people who were about to take their first offensive action ever against the invaders couldn't have asked for a more suitable battlefield.

Dan had assigned himself to one of the end groups, so that he wouldn't have to arrange for a signal to be given simultaneously to both flanks; the group across from him would move into action immediately after he led his own group to the shoreline. And the time to do that was now.

He gestured toward the water, started crawling in that direction, and four other people did the same. He poked his head out of the thick grass at the edge of the pond and waited for a couple of tense minutes until he saw another head on the opposite shore. Then all ten of the first-line "shakers," five on one side and five on the other, went into action at the same time.

Using hands protected by rubber gloves or patches of rubber that had been tied and stitched into makeshift coverings, they grabbed the planks they had carried with them and silently dipped them into the water. Then, trying to be quiet and quick about it at the same time, they started to paddle gently, setting up a couple of wave motions directed at oblique angles toward the part of the shore farthest from the monsters.

The manufactured currents caused the floating powwers to begin drifting, moving with agonizing slowness toward where the "movers" — the net teams — waited. When the floating silver discs had been forced into a fairly small cluster by the action of the waves, the movers would run out of hiding, fling out their nets, and haul them back in with a full load of the strangest quarry anyone on Earth had ever fished for.

Dan froze as, before his eyes, two powwers floated into contact with each other and a sharp, crackling noise split the air. Before he could even think about moving for safety, his eyes flicked to the right. The monsters had not moved; either they didn't hear the noise — which he thought unlikely — or they didn't care. He reasoned that these things must brush up against each other in the water all the time; maybe this sort of "sparking" was of no concern to the creatures. He resumed paddling, and the others, following his lead, did the same.

The shakers pulled back after paddling for thirty seconds, enough time to set up waves that would not dissipate until they had served their purpose. As he yanked his head back inside the safety of the marsh grass, Dan exhaled — and realized he hadn't taken a breath in quite some time. He parted the strands of grass in front of his face to get a look at the soon-to-begin netting operation. And then all hell broke loose.

First, a *whump* — a noise that sounded like pressurized air being released through a wide opening. Then, a second later, an explosion and a gout of flame on the opposite shore. One person screamed, and another one's body was thrown a short distance and landed dangling head down in the water, submerged to the chest.

The placid marsh literally exploded in a dozen places at once as more explosives rained down along the shoreline. The monsters *had* been alerted by the crackling noise — it had just taken them a few seconds to load, aim, and fire their weapons.

"Some of those things still have power left!" Dan cried, hardly able to believe that the aliens were turning their weapons on him and his group.

Nearly insane with panic, Dan still had the good sense not to stand up. A man and a woman who did show themselves, a few yards to his left, died before they could run three steps. A sizzling beam of coherent light hit the man in the upper back, came out the left side of his chest, and burned a hole through the woman's skull an instant later.

"Back!" Dan yelled at the top of his lungs as he started to crawl away from the pond. Then he realized the order couldn't be heard above the explosions and screams, and in any event it was superfluous — nobody was going to stay put and risk getting blown to bits.

When he got far enough away to feel reasonably safe, Dan turned and, on his knees, tried to assess the situation. The grenades were coming down in a tight ring around the pond, but none of them were hitting the water. It seemed that the xenoborgs were mainly concerned about protecting the powwers; they wanted the people to get away from the shore but didn't care if the survivors escaped back into the woods.

Okay, he thought. We can fall back and live to fight another time. We can—

Dan's jaw dropped in shock as he saw six people burst out of the grass along the far shore, one of them carrying a net. Then terror stabbed his heart as he recognized who was leading the way: it was Kirk — and Karen was there, too! Dan's first impulse was to rush toward them and force them back under cover, tackling and dragging them if he had to. But he immediately realized there was no way he could reach them in time to prevent what they were about to do.

Kirk stopped at the edge of the shore and unfolded the net into a long cylinder, passing the ends to a woman on his left and a man on his right. They in turn opened it up even more, passing it to the people who had lined up beside them. Karen was on the end farthest from Dan, a good sixty yards from where he was crouched, and he strained to keep an eye on her while he prayed for her safety. In unison, the six of them dropped the leading edge of the huge, rectangular net at their feet and took a short step forward to secure it against the ground while they held onto the opposite edge.

Then, with surprising smoothness and speed considering their lack of experience and the danger they were in, they unfurled the net and grabbed the other edge. Karen and the man on the extreme other end of the line also pulled out and anchored under their feet a pair of long cords attached to the corners of the net. The six people bent over and then straightened up abruptly, throwing their arms out and releasing the net when their hands reached waist height. The net's edge, weighted with lead shot and the insulating rubber, sailed more than twenty feet through the air before settling over the pond. As soon as the weighted edge hit the water, it sank a few inches below the surface — trapping about three dozen of the silver things beneath the mesh.

Grenades were going off intermittently all around them, and still they worked. Karen and the man who had anchored the other cord picked up the free ends of those lines and began pulling on them, dragging the submerged far edge of the net back toward the netters. The others stooped and lifted the edge they had been standing on, then began backing up with short, choppy steps, pulling quickly but carefully, helping to haul the net and the powwers within it closer to shore. Crackling and popping noises had abounded when the net came into contact with the electrified discs, but that was nothing compared to the commotion caused when the net dragged all of the powwers into one silver-colored heap. The very air seemed alive with electricity as the things all shorted out against one another. Dan, looking on terrified and transfixed, was amazed that the people pulling the net could find the courage to keep on dragging the mass toward shore when it seemed as though the whole pile of powwers might explode or incinerate themselves any second.

The group was about ten feet away from the shore, with another ten or fifteen feet to go before the net would be completely hauled in. Suddenly, an explosion tore up the ground a few feet behind where Kirk was standing. He and the people on either side of him were thrown toward the pond by the concussion from the blast.

They survived the explosion, and probably weren't even seriously hurt by it. But when they landed, all three of them were sprawled out across the mesh of the net — the part that wasn't insulated. The bodies twitched reflexively for a couple of seconds and then were still.

That was all Dan could take. He erupted from his hiding place with a guttural scream and began running in a gradual arc that would bring him to where Karen was standing. She and the two other surviving netters tugged frantically at the rubberized edge for a few seconds, but they couldn't possibly move the net any farther with the weight of three human beings on top of it. She dropped her part of the net and turned to run for cover just as Dan opened his mouth to call out to her.

Karen stopped in her tracks and hit the ground. Dan thought she had been hurt, but then he saw what she had seen. A Cyborg Commando was racing out of the woods and toward the pond! No . . . not one — there were four of them!

In four different places along the far side of the pond they appeared. When they reached places where they had a clear view of the monsters lined up about fifty yards away, they dropped on their stomachs, extended their arms, and began firing. Laser beams shot across the intervening distance millions of times faster than the eye could follow. Dan tore his gaze from the shooters and looked toward the creatures. Every beam was aimed at one of the largest xenoborgs in the line, and every beam hit its target.

Four of the monsters literally exploded, spewing flesh over the still-motionless insects closest to them. Dan guessed, correctly, that laser shots had hit grenades that these creatures hadn't used yet. For the other aliens that were hit, death came more slowly but just as surely as their bulbous bodies were scorched again and again by the narrow beams.

In less than a minute, it was over. No more grenades fell from the sky. The powwers, although they hadn't been pulled completely out of the water, had stopped giving off crackling and popping noises. The smaller xenoborgs and insects that hadn't been killed — yet — remained unmoving. Dan wondered, with loathing and utter disdain, whether they were even aware of what had just happened.

When he was sure the silence was going to last, he ran toward Karen once again. The four CCs had gotten to their feet and were moving around, checking for wounded people and helping to get the group reorganized.

"Oh, God!" Dan breathed, choking back a sob as he embraced Karen. "I'm so glad you're alive! You never should have—"

"Kirk!" Karen said frantically. She pulled away from him far enough to see around him and get a glimpse of where the net was spread along the shoreline. "Help him, Dan!"

He took her by the upper arms and turned her toward him again. "He's dead, Karen. All three of them. . . ." She started to break down, and he shook her gently in an effort to snap her out of it. "Why did you do it?" he asked. The question might have waited, but he had to know.

"It was him," she said through her tears. "Kirk. He wouldn't run — he said he'd put the net out by himself if he had to. And we couldn't . . . we couldn't let him do that."

"What you did took a lot of courage," he said softly, hoping the praise would console her.

"No," she said. "I wasn't brave — I was scared! I was so afraid. . . ."

One of the cyborgs, passing within earshot, stepped over and put a hand on Karen's shoulder. "I'm scared every minute of every day," he said to her. "It's nothing to be ashamed of."

Dan recognized the voice. It was one of the CCs who had first told them about the plan — the one that his companion had called "the corporal."

"It's good to see you again," he said, holding out his hand. "And . . . thanks."

"Sorry we couldn't get here sooner," Richard said. "We're a roving patrol, supposed to step in and help out wherever we can. We were a few miles away when we heard the explosions start, and—"

"And you got here in less than five minutes?" Dan interrupted.

Richard let the question, obviously a rhetorical one, pass. Just then Cris strode up to where the three of them were standing.

"Cris, this is Dan," said Richard. "Part of the group Tony and I talked to on that first day by the highway, when you were—"

"I remember you telling me about him." Cris turned to Dan and added, "They tell me you're in charge here."

"I was, anyway," he answered. "After this, they'll probably want someone else to make the decisions."

"What do you mean, 'after this'? I was just about to congratulate you."

"For what? At least six people are dead—"

"And a few hundred creatures are either dead, or soon to be, because of what you people accomplished. It sounds callous as hell, but try to understand: If we can kill two hundred invaders for every six people we lose, we're going to win this war and win it quickly. Don't diminish the deaths of those people by telling yourself they died for nothing — because that's not true."

"He's right, Dan," said Karen, her voice calm and strong. "We're not all going to get through this alive — but we all have to keep fighting, for the sake of those who do survive. Am I making any sense?"

"You sure are," he said after a pause, then turned to Cris. "And you do, too. We are going to win, aren't we?"

"I'd bet my life on it," said Cris solemnly.

22

April 14, 2037

Ryan Murphy had not been pleased in the least when his father and most of the other adults at the Larson home headed out to, as he put it, "kill the power-things."

About an hour before the group was scheduled to leave, Dan had taken his son aside and tried to prepare him for their upcoming separation. He was surprised by Ryan's response.

"I thought I was gonna get to go with," he said petulantly. "I want to help kill the power-things, and I thought—"

"I'm very proud of you, guy," Dan said, meaning every word. He had expected Ryan to react strongly to the prospect of being separated from his father, but that objection was apparently a secondary one. The boy was genuinely disappointed about not being allowed a chance to contribute. "You've really grown up in a hurry," Dan continued, and then added to himself, But now I want you to keep growing. . . .

"Then why can't I go?" he asked. "I can help pull a net. I can be a lookout. I can do lots of things."

Dan tried a white lie, something he hoped the boy wouldn't be able to double-check later, and got away with it. "The people who are telling the rest of us what to do decided that somebody should stay behind to keep the young children safe, and to help Mr. and Mrs. Larson.

"That's an important job, too, and you're the best one we could think of to do it."

That last statement wasn't far from the truth, and because of that Dan could say it with enough conviction to make Ryan accept it.

When the adults and teenagers left to take their places in the field, Ryan would be the oldest and strongest child on the premises. Of the fifteen other people who would stay behind, two were the owners of the house, six — including Suzie Peters — were women with young children, and the other seven were the children themselves, none of them more than five years old.

"I understand," said Ryan in a low voice, partly because he actually did and partly because he realized he wasn't going to change his father's mind anyway. "I'll do the best I can," he added, and even managed a small smile to go along with it.

"I know you will," Dan said, putting his arms around the boy. "We all will."

* * *

That had been four days ago. In the meantime, Ryan had proven his value to the group at the Larson home time and time again. He accepted without complaint the responsibility for mundane tasks such as getting water — and with so many people in the house, a bucket or two of water didn't last long. He met the challenges of doing things, big and small, that he had never done before. He put clean diapers on babies and washed out the soiled ones. He helped Andrew hang a door on a long-unused upstairs bedroom — "something I never coulda done by myself," the old man said, tousling Ryan's hair when the job was done.

He kept watch over toddlers so their mothers could rest or get their other chores done, and he learned at an early age that it takes a lot of energy to keep up with a two-year-old and a lot of patience to keep one happy. He kept one little girl from getting seriously hurt when he ran across the kitchen and scooped her up into his arms just before she took a tumble down the basement stairs.

All the adults were grateful for his help and spared no effort to make sure he knew that. He enjoyed the praise and the small rewards that came with it — a hug, a tender touch — but he was never completely happy. He wasn't doing what he really wanted to do.

Andrew Larson could sense the boy's mood, and when it hadn't changed after four days he decided a little chat was in order. When all the younger children were bedded down that night, he tapped Ryan on the shoulder and motioned for the boy to follow him out to the front porch.

"Thought you'd like t' sit for a while and have some man-ta-man talk," Andrew began. "We got a lot in common, y' know."

"You mean like, we're both men?"

"Yeah, but more than that. We're two men with the same problem."

"What's that?"

"Well, I don't know about you, but I'd sure like t' be out there right now, pullin' up those power-things and helpin' get rid of those zee-no-borgs."

"Me too!" said Ryan. "I was gonna go, but—"

"But it's not a job for folks like us," Andrew said realistically, sadly. "Somebody's gotta take care of those people inside, and we were the best ones for that."

"Yeah. That's what my dad said. I was the best one to stay behind, he said."

"Well, he was right. I don't know what we woulda done without you around here the last few days."

"I like helping," Ryan said. "It makes me feel good. But I'd feel even better if I could stay here for a while and then go help fight the xenoborgs."

"I know what y' mean. Sure would be nice to smack one of 'em right between the eyes, wouldn't it?"

"They don't have eyes," said Ryan, taking advantage of the chance to show off his knowledge.

"They got heads?" said Andrew with a chuckle.

"Ummm . . . sort of, I guess."

"Then we'd knock 'em over the head, eyes or no eyes! Right?"

"Right!" said Ryan enthusiastically, caught up in the moment.

Andrew was suddenly afraid that he had gone too far. Maybe he'll get it in his head to run off and do something foolish, the man thought. Hell, he'd probably have a better chance against one of 'em than I would, but he's still got no business out there. . . .

"But what we'd like t' do and what we have t' do are two different things, and we have t' be satisfied to help in what ways we can," Andrew said, leaning toward the boy for emphasis and then asking, "You understand, don't you?"

"Yes, sir," Ryan lied, sensing that this would not be a good time to tell the old man how he really felt.

"Now we better get our rest." The old man rose slowly and headed for the front door.

"Okay," said Ryan, subdued. He went to his bed, on the living-room floor, but he didn't get much rest. For a long time after the old man had taken to snoring in his bedroom above where Ryan lay, the child stayed awake and thought about all the things he would do to the loathsome creatures if he ever got the chance.

* * *

It was still dark when Ryan woke up with a start. A noise . . . and there it was again. A scratching noise, coming from outside the kitchen window. Someone, or something, was trying to get in!

He got up and moved quickly to the two women who were sleeping in the living room along with their youngsters. By the time he woke one of them, the other was stirring. The scratching noise was continuing, a new sound every few seconds. And now some of the scratches were accompanied by something that sounded like the splintering of wood.

Fighting back his panic, Ryan bounded halfway up the stairs leading to the bedrooms. "Wake up!" he shouted. "Wake up! Something's outside!"

Suzie was the first to appear at the top of the stairs, clutching a still-sleeping Jacob. "What is it?" she said drowsily.

"Something's outside!" he repeated. "Monsters, I think!"

Almost simultaneously the other bedroom doors opened. Pulling on his robe as he lumbered toward the stairs, Andrew Larson took charge. "Everybody downstairs!" he ordered. "In the basement!"

No one wasted any time in complying . . . except Ryan. He returned to the living room and held back while the others ran through the kitchen, carrying children or pulling them by the hand, and descended the basement stairs as fast as they could.

"C'mon, Ryan!" yelled Andrew as he headed for the kitchen doorway. The scratching noises had now become crunching sounds, and they were coming from the wall adjacent to the kitchen window they would have to run past to make it to the basement. "Now!" the old man bellowed. He took two steps toward the boy and would have chased him down and grabbed him if Ryan had not decided to move.

They got past the wall that was apparently being torn down from outside. Andrew pulled Ryan in front of him as they neared the stairs, but when the boy got to the landing he stopped again.

"Keep going!" the old man ordered.

"But we have to fight it!" said Ryan, suddenly breaking free of the old man's grasp. "We were left to take care of these people, and if we don't do something, that thing's going to eat its way inside this house and we'll all be dead!"

The crunching sounds grew louder, and plaster began to crumble as the unseen intruder gnawed its way into the wall.

"Now's our chance, Mister Larson. Knock 'em over the head — remember?" Ryan tried to get the old man moving.

Andrew Larson was seventy years his senior, but the look in Ryan Murphy's eyes was something the old man had seen only seldom in his lifetime. It was a look that said, This is what I have to do, with you or without you. He paused a second longer and then decided.

"You're somethin', boy. You're somethin'." Andrew reached up, grabbed a battery-powered lantern from the shelf next to him, and flicked it on. "We gotta get to the tool shed. Follow me."

After pausing at the back door to be sure nothing was right outside, Andrew pushed the door open and started to trot the fifty feet to the shed as fast as he could. Ryan could have covered the distance in less than half the time, but he stayed by the man's side.

"Can you handle a pitchfork?" Andrew asked as he surveyed the weapons they had to choose from.

"I can lift it, if that's what you mean."

"Okay," the man said, peering around, looking for something in particular. "Ah, this'll do me," he said, picking up an axe with his free hand. "Now, let's go see what that critter is made of."

The only sound in the still night air other than their muffled footsteps was the incessant scratching and crunching, coming from the single spot where Ryan had first noticed it. At least we don't have to worry about getting surrounded, Andrew thought.

He turned off the lantern and put it on the ground as they left the tool shed. Andrew bent to whisper in Ryan's ear. "Real slow and real quiet. When we get around the corner, put that fork in front o' you and stab anywhere you can hit it."

The sound was less intense out here than it had been from inside the house, but there was still no mistaking where it was coming from. They crept to the corner of the outside wall, knowing that five or six feet away on the other side was the thing they had come to kill. Andrew Larson, having come this far, saw no point in wasting time.

"Now!" he whispered, moving as quickly as he could around the corner and bringing the axe into striking position. An instant later, Ryan darted out to a spot about five feet to the man's left.

The thing was not a xenoborg. It was much smaller, and it had a hard, shiny outer shell. It was black, but readily visible in the moonlight. It was a beetle — a beetle two feet tall and five feet long!

If the thing was aware of their presence, it gave no indication. It kept scratching and clawing with its powerful pincers, pulling itself up to a leaning position against the wall and then trying to rip and tear pieces of wood as its front end fell back to the ground.

Andrew made a circling motion with his left arm,

and Ryan interpreted it correctly, giving the back end of the creature a wide berth as he moved around to its left flank. He waited, not sure what would happen if he darted forward and jabbed the fork into the thing. And it was a good thing he did.

Andrew Larson took three calculated steps toward the right rear section of the beetle's body, planted his foot, raised the axe over his head, and brought it down on the creature. The blade cut through the carapace easily. A brief spray of fluid spurted out of the wound, and then thick liquid began to ooze from the opening as Andrew pulled the axe head free.

In that same instant, the creature turned with surprising speed to face its attacker, forgetting all about the wall it had been trying to demolish. Ryan ran forward, holding the pitchfork at waist height parallel to the ground, and drove the tines into the creature's left side.

That made it react in the opposite direction, thrashing its pincers back toward the left and causing its head to thud into the wall as it did so. In the space of those few seconds, Andrew and Ryan had come up with an unbeatable plan of attack. They simply alternated blows on the thing, bringing it closer to death each time the axe or the fork penetrated. Confused and physically traumatized, trapped between its assailants and the wall, the thing had no chance.

Both of them continued to stab it and chop at it

for several minutes after the thing had become motionless. If an ordinary bug stopped moving, you could be sure it was dead — but this was no ordinary bug. As they continued to attack, the old man and the boy cheered each other on. And when they were sure it was over, they sat down on the grass together for a moment before going back inside.

"We got our chance," said Ryan, looking up with admiration at the old man as both of them struggled to get their breathing and heartbeats back to normal.

"Yep, we sure did!" said Andrew Larson, smiling at the boy. "And I never coulda done it by myself."

They leaned toward each other, reached out, and embraced — seventy years apart in age, but as close in spirit as two people could ever be.

23

April 19, 2037

Operation Manpower was officially called off eight days after it had begun. They were eight days that had changed the course of the world more than any other event in human history — indeed, that had made it possible for the world to continue to exist.

The xenoborgs and insects were beaten. Not killed off yet, but unmistakably beaten. Once deprived of the energy they needed to operate their weapons and devices, the leader-type xenoborgs were just as easy to kill as their smaller, unadorned counterparts. Cyborg Commando squads roamed the front lines of every battle across the planet, slicing and blasting xenoborgs with virtual impunity whenever they encountered a group of monsters that had been rendered powwerless.

Right up until the minute when the scales tipped irrevocably in favor of the human race, the Operation Manpower assault teams remained in the forefront of the struggle. The people suffered enormous losses; more than a few teams were killed down to the last man or woman. But whenever a team was crippled or wiped out, another one would move in to fill the breach.

No one wanted to die; all the people, except for a fanatical few, lived in fear for every minute of every day while the operation was in progress. But that didn't keep them from doing what they had come to do. In the months that followed, memorials and statues would be erected in hundreds of places around the world. Some of them were put up at spots in the wilderness where dozens of people had died in a single conflict. Others were located in cities and towns that had not been the scenes of battles, where they were seen or visited by thousands of people every day. Those who had lived through the invasion and its aftermath would never forget the sacrifice that thousands of others had made. They didn't *want* to forget, and they would pass that attitude along to generations yet unborn.

The military leaders around the world — those administering the Cyborg Commando Force as well as those in charge of conventional armies — were universally awed at how well Operation Manpower had worked. In part, the success was due to simple good fortune. Ultimately, the enemy's rampage of destruction actually helped to bring about the quick victory; the advancing force thinned out as it moved and broke into smaller groups that could more easily be headed off and challenged by the humans and CCs. By the third day of Operation Manpower, the lines of xenoborgs and insects were fragmented and in disarray. Stories began to circulate about how ordinary people, armed only with clubs and farm implements, had attacked and killed solitary insects or small groups of them that were discovered meandering in the countryside.

Another bit of good luck: As many of the assault squads had quickly found out, it wasn't always necessary to drag the powwers completely out of the water. If the floating silver things were attacked fairly late in the day, after each of them had built up a sizable store of electrical energy, they could be rendered useless by simply forcing them into contact with each other and causing them to short out.

Every little bit of new information that was transmitted back to the military strategists made them more and more confident that the plan would succeed. But instead of sitting back and congratulating themselves for being such fine planners, they silently praised the real heroes — the people who were working . . . and dying . . . to make the victory attainable.

The reaction of General Garrison, monitoring

status reports back at the Manitowoc base, was typical. "Amazing," he would mutter at various times, usually just after receiving news of another series of successful assaults. The word was inappropriate, because what he felt was not amazement but awe and respect, and those feelings came through in the way he uttered it. "These people are . . . amazing." The officers around him murmured their agreement or nodded silently. Nothing more needed to be said.

* * *

Cris, Maura, Tony, and Richard walked into a small briefing room where Traynor sat awaiting them. The man jumped to his feet, as though they were the authority figures instead of he.

"Welcome back," he said, sounding like a father whose children had just come home after a long absence. Then, in a reaction that was as appreciated as it was uncharacteristic, he approached the CCs one at a time and clumsily embraced them.

"God, it's nice to be home," said Tony as he flopped overdramatically into a chair. "I never thought I'd be happy to see these cream-colored walls, but I sure do feel *good* right now."

"So," Cris said lightly, "what's next?" He knew the worst of the fighting was over, and now he was actually looking forward to getting new orders. Whatever they were, they were bound to be easier, less dangerous, than what they had just helped to accomplish.

"That depends," Traynor said with a grin.

"On what?" Tony asked, pulling himself into an upright sitting position. "Are we going to get a chance to choose our next assignment?"

"Let the man talk," Maura said, in a tone of voice her three companions had become accustomed to. She had a feeling that something . . . unusual . . . was about to happen.

"Obviously," Traynor went on, "things outside are going very well. If that wasn't the case, you'd still be out there. But what you may not realize is just *how* well things are going.

"Operation Manpower has been discontinued. The people have done their jobs. What we have left now is nothing more than a mop-up operation. As you know from experience, the remaining xenoborgs and the giant insects are defenseless against Cyborg Commandos. The most difficult part about killing them is finding them, because once we locate them, they're dead meat.

"And even finding them isn't very tough, because for the first time in more than two years we have control of the air again. Regular infantry and artillery, combined with aerial reconnaissance, can now accomplish what only CCs used to be able to do. Reports of successful engagements against xenoborgs and insects are coming in almost faster than we can process them, and the situation is basically the same in every other area of the world."

Traynor paused for effect. A wide smile spread across his face, and he added, "What I'm saying, people, is that we don't need you any more."

Maura clutched Cris's hand, and no one broke the silence for a few seconds as the full meaning of Traynor's words sank in. Then Cris said, hesitantly and hopefully, "You mean . . . ?"

"I mean the only thing standing between you and an honorable discharge from the Cyborg Commando Force is a small pile of paperwork. You've all been in those bodies longer than most of the rest of the force, and seniority does have its privileges. You can get out any time you want."

Another brief silence descended over the group. Then Traynor, realizing the inaccuracy of what he had just said, turned toward Richard Adams. The expression on the man's face conveyed his thoughts.

"I didn't mean—"

"No need to apologize," Richard said to Traynor. "What you said is true — it's just that I'm not in a position to take advantage of the opportunity.

"In spite of that," he continued, "I always hoped I'd live to see this moment. It means we won. Life can go on. Things can be like before. . . ."

"Things will never be like before," said Cris somberly. "Not for any of us, and especially not for you. But we'll make the best of it."

"Exactly," said Richard. "I've always known that my brain doesn't have a body to go back to. Thanks to you people, I was able to come to terms with that fact. I've accepted it, and I'll deal with it. There's still something I can do — right, sir?"

"Absolutely," the man replied. "With that body and that frame of mind, you can do anything you want."

"Well," Tony interjected, "I guess you talked us into it."

"Us?"

"Yeah. Remember what you said — we can get out any time we want. Well, knowing that is enough for me right now. Maybe someday I'll decide to resume occupancy of the body I was born in, but for now, at least, I think I'd like to stay in the service. Maybe you guys could find something for Richard and me to do together, if that's okay with him. . . ."

"I'll insist on it," said Richard.

"And so will I," replied Traynor. "You two deserve each other," he said with a warm smile and a chuckle, recalling the day in his office when Tony and Richard had practically come to blows. My, how things have changed, he thought. . . .

"Okay, that's settled," Tony said brightly. "Now, what about you?" he added, gesturing with a flourish toward Cris and Maura.

Both of them seemed reluctant to answer at first, and then they started to talk at the same time.

"I'll go along with—" Cris began.

"You decide for us," said Maura on top of his words.

"Aw, come on," Tony said, breaking the tension. "I think you both know what you want, and I think it's the same thing. So *say* it!"

"We want to get out," Cris said, giving Maura's hand a squeeze.

"Bring on the paperwork," Maura added.

Traynor smirked. "The paperwork is done," he said. "All we need are your signatures, and you'll be on your way out."

"But . . ." Cris stammered. "How did you . . . ?"

Maura put an arm around Cris's shoulders and looked at Traynor. "I think he had a feeling," she said.

* * *

Ryan, on his way back from an excursion for water, was the first to see the group coming toward the house. His heart leaped at the sight of the human figures that had just topped the crest of the hill. He strained to see if one of them was his father. But all he could see was that there were about twenty people — half of the number that had left from here. And they were still too far away to identify.

"Someone's coming!" Ryan yelled as he ran up to the house and dropped the bucket he had been lugging, spilling most of its contents in the process. Before anyone could stop him, the boy took off toward the approaching group.

Dan was walking in silence next to Karen, his hand grasping hers tightly. It took him a few seconds to notice the small figure running at top speed through the field and straight for them. "Ryan!" Dan yelled when he realized there was only one person that size who would be coming from the direction of the Larson home. He dropped Karen's hand and took off running, tears streaming down his face. He had almost been afraid to come back to the Larson home, after hearing that some wandering insects had ravaged several of the farms in the area. His heart had been heavy throughout the journey back. But now it soared higher than it had in a very long time.

"Dad! Daddy!" Ryan screamed gleefully, recognizing his father about the same time Dan saw him. And in the interminable seconds that it took the father and son to close the gap between them, Ryan's eyes became flooded with tears of overwhelming relief.

"You're safe! You're safe!" Ryan repeated the words, almost as though he couldn't believe they were true, as he flung himself into his father's open arms.

"Oh, guy, you don't know how glad I am to see you!" Dan cried, grabbing hold of the boy and wrapping his arms around the happy child.

"Wait 'til you hear what Andrew and I did — all by ourselves," Ryan said proudly, after the emotional reunion was over. "We killed the biggest beetle you ever saw!"

"Oh, yeah? You and Andrew? All by yourselves?" Dan asked, his voice full of pride and emotion.

"Yup, we did," Ryan said with an equal amount of pride.

"Well, you two will have to tell me all about it. And I have a few stories for you, too," Dan said. At that moment Karen and Jerry came up behind Ryan and Dan.

"Hi, guy!" Karen said, her eyes moist. "I'm so happy to see that you're okay." Dan took her hand.

"I'm glad you and Jerry are fine, too," Ryan said sincerely, and then asked, "Where's Kirk?"

The three adults exchanged glances. Dan was the first to speak. "Kirk was a very brave boy, Ryan. Just like you. He and others like him have helped to make sure that we won't have to hide any more."

"He's dead, isn't he?" Ryan asked quietly.

"Yes, I'm afraid so," Dan answered, his voice equally subdued.

"I wish I could see him one more time so I could tell him how brave I think he is and . . ." Ryan paused momentarily before continuing. "And that I think he would have made a wonderful brother."

"We'll never forget him," Karen said softly.

"Or his sacrifice," Jerry added.

They enjoyed the rest of that walk toward the farmhouse, where other members of their extended family stood waiting. This was the first time in as long as he could remember that Dan had experienced the pleasure of walking through a field without having to fear what might suddenly appear on the horizon.

Those waiting back on the porch of the Larson home cheered as the group came into view. There would be a lot of mourning but even more celebrating to be done in the days ahead. Almost everyone left alive would feel a new sense of kinship with his fellow human beings, giving a new meaning to the old expression "brotherhood of man." There would be a lot of rebuilding to do. But after what they had just gone through, that would seem easy and almost enjoyable.

They had weathered a storm so devastating that the only thing that had kept them alive had been their refusal to simply lie down and die. They had reason to feel proud — yes, maybe even invincible. They had fought for it, and they had won the ultimate prize.

24

May 4, 2037

Cris Holman was aware. Aware of the fact that he was aware of . . . everything!

I . . . AM . . . ALIVE!

Those three words were the first conscious thought that had originated in Cris's brain since shortly before his cybernetic body had been powered down in preparation for the operation. He was alive . . . which meant—

I AM . . . HUMAN!

Although neither his vocal cords nor his tongue were functional yet, Cris Holman's brain, which now rested comfortably inside his human skull, fairly shouted that news as, one after another, and sometimes one on top of the other, old, long-forgotten sensations rushed in to reintroduce themselves.

I . . . CAN . . . FEEL!

As his brain struggled to regain control of the body it had been born in, to recall all of the commands necessary to begin the operation of Cris Holman's human parts, it also fought to wrench itself from the tenacious grasp of sensations and memories from another time — a time it wanted to, but could not, entirely forget.

I . . . HURT!

Cris moaned inwardly, wondering how he had ever withstood such gruesome unpleasantness before his transformation into a cybernetic soldier, before his existence inside a body that could not feel pain. It had been two years and several months since he had felt any true physical sensations. But it didn't take long for him to refamiliarize himself with the feelings of pain, cold, and hunger, as all three came back in a mad rush, as though each was competing for top billing in his nervous system.

He had been drifting in and out of consciousness for the last three hours, and he was uncertain about how much of what went through his brain had been verbalized and how much had been simply thought or dreamed.

HOW MUCH OF THIS IS REAL?

Cris found himself wondering if the alien invasion had been nothing more than a horrible nightmare. Maybe he was really still in Delavan, having his usual trouble trying to force himself to wakefulness after a good night's sleep. Maybe Sara would come bouncing through the door any minute, pull the covers off his sleepy frame, and demand him to "Get up, you lazy bum!" Maybe his father and stepmother were in the kitchen, chatting over coffee, and all he would have to do was wake up so he could go join them.

God! What was happening here? What was real? What wasn't?

He suddenly felt very foolish as he remembered the part of the dream where he played the hero, attempting to save his world and all of its inhabitants. When he first started to regain consciousness, he actually thought he had just undergone surgery to regain his human status after serving as some kind of super hero!

WAKE UP!

Cris tried to will himself to full consciousness,

but he seemed to be no closer to throwing his feet over the side of the bed and setting them in motion on the floor than he had been a few minutes earlier. So instead, he continued to fantasize about waking up.

THAT'S IT! I'M JUST ASLEEP! NONE OF WHAT I JUST THOUGHT ABOUT IS REAL!

But Cris Holman's joy quickly turned to horror as in his mind's eye he saw a huge, tentacled monster grab his sister Sara and start to engulf her body.

No! No!

He tried to scream, but no sound came out. It *was* a nightmare — and all he had to do to make it go away was wake up! He consoled himself with that fact and tried to remain calm while waiting for Sara to rouse him from this unholiest of unconscious existences.

He tried to remain calm as legions of huge, ghastly creatures paraded through his mind.

YOU'RE NOT REAL! I JUST DREAMED YOU!

Cris screamed at the ugly mob of monsters, which turned, suddenly, and began moving in his direction. One horrible mass, thousands of bodies of alien flesh that moved as one — it was after him!

GO AWAY!

Dream or no dream, this was more than Cris's brain could handle. Out of instinct, he raised his arms and extended them into attack position. He played his laser beams back and forth, up and down along each creature's bulbous body.

NOW YOU DIE!

Cris screamed the words over and over again. But nothing happened. No beams of coherent light projected from his outthrust arms. There were no chopped-up bits of alien flesh lying in the street in front of him.

OH, NO! I MUST BE OUT OF POWER!

Cris lowered his arms and retreated, leading the group of hungry aliens to the edge of a high precipice. Cris looked back over his shoulder and stopped. There was no more ground to back up over. Behind him was only open space, and a drop that seemed to descend into the deepest pit of hell.

Cris turned and faced the angry mob, which was now no more than a few feet away from him and was still pressing forward. He faced his palms toward the horde, training his microwave projectors on the front section of the closest alien, and attempted to call up a full power, narrow-beam shot of radiation from each sweaty palm. But instead of popping and sizzling, the thing just kept advancing until it was close enough to reach out a tentacle and begin encircling Cris's human body.

No! No!

Cris screamed and writhed frantically, managing to pull himself free. But his freedom was short-lived, for in the next instant Cris Holman felt himself falling off the edge of the earth, his body helplessly descending into the pit of fire far below.

"AAAAEEEEEE. . . ."

"It's all right, Mr. Holman. You're all right now." An unfamiliar voice tried to reassure Cris as he struggled to open his eyes. As his human eyes began to focus, he realized that the face that went with the voice was also unfamiliar.

"I was right. It *was* a dream!" Cris said, still very groggy. And then, his consciousness suddenly returning in full force, he fired off three questions in rapid succession. "Who are you? What are you doing in my bedroom? Where's Sara?"

"Relax, Mr. Holman. You're going to be fine. You've just undergone a very complicated operation, and you must give yourself more time to fully wake up. I'm going to get someone to help you." And with that, the mysterious person left his bedroom. Only . . .

This wasn't his bedroom. And that meant it hadn't been a dream — not all of it, anyway. Cris's memory was suddenly working very well. So well, in fact, that now he seemed to be recalling everything at once. And the pain . . .

The pain — a good sign! He was whole again! His head throbbed worse than he would have thought possible. His body felt stiff and it ached all over . . . but it was *his* body!

"It worked," he shouted hoarsely, as loud as he could.

"It certainly did!" This time the voice was a familiar one.

"Traynor . . ." said Cris, dropping the volume of his voice as he relaxed slightly. "You did it! I'm me again!" Cris Holman enjoyed the sensation of being able to feel the corners of his mouth as they moved slowly upward. He tried to lift his arm, but it was like lifting a barrel of lead.

"Take it easy," Traynor commanded. "Your body has been out of commission a very long time. It's about as weak as you would imagine, considering it hasn't been exercised for a couple of years."

"Yeah, I guess I should have figured it would be," Cris said sheepishly. "Looks like my next ten years are going to be spent in a rehab center."

"Don't worry. You'll be surprised how quickly you're able to get back into shape again. Before you know it, you'll be doing all the things you did before."

"I don't suppose you left any of my laser blasters intact." Cris winked, and felt a quiet thrill at the feeling of being able to open and close his eyes.

"Sorry, kid. You couldn't harm a rabbit with those fingers now. You're nothing but plain old flesh and blood again."

"I think I can live with that," Cris said happily.

"I'm extremely happy to hear that, Cris," Traynor said seriously. "A very large number of former CCs — more than we anticipated, I'm afraid — have been having a hard time adjusting to their old, less-than-superhuman selves."

"Hey, don't worry about me! As long as those things are gone, I just want to be myself again," Cris answered with equal seriousness.

"Good. Now, we want you to rest and get all the sleep you can. Your body has been through a tremendous shock. You have to give it plenty of time to readjust. Then, when we think you're up to it, we'll brief you—" Traynor interrupted his own monologue with an embarrassed grin. "In a couple of days we'll *talk to* you about the therapy you'll be undergoing. But before you doze off again, there's someone who'd like to see you."

Without another word, Traynor walked over and opened the door of Cris's hospital room. For a few seconds no one appeared in the doorway. And then, very slowly, with no small amount of effort, Maura Woolsey walked over the threshold, her frail body supported by crutches strapped under her arms.

"Maura!" Cris yelled, trying to raise his head off the pillow. His face contorted with pain, but his head didn't move from its soft resting place.

"Not so fast, hotshot," his fiancée said softly. "It takes a few hours of recuperation before you'll be able to pull off that little stunt. It takes longer than that to be able to do what I'm doing. But it does come back, Cris, and a whole lot faster than I would have thought."

"Oh Maura, I'm so happy you're all right," Cris cried. And then, her words suddenly hitting home, he asked, "But how long have you been conscious? We went under at approximately the same time. I don't understand."

"It just proves something man has known since the beginning of time," she said, giving Cris a mischievous look. "When it comes to the human race, the female sex is definitely stronger."

Traynor leaned over and addressed Cris in a stage whisper. "Don't listen to her. If it hadn't been for the fact that she happened to regain consciousness two days earlier than you did—"

"Like I said, women are—"

"Two days?" Cris interrupted.

"Aggravating as hell!" Traynor cut in, finishing

Maura's pronouncement. Then he added, "I'm going to leave you alone with her for a while, Cris. But if she gives you any trouble, let me know."

Traynor winked and left the room.

Cris just stared at Maura, who by this time had made it to the side of his bed and was preparing to sit down beside his prone body. That accomplished, she reached for his hand and held it as tightly as she was able. "Looks like these fingers will have to spend some time squeezing rubber balls before they'll be able to perform as well as they used to. I think a few other parts of my body are going to need a rigorous workout, too," she said softly.

"Hey, I don't care about your grip. And I don't give a damn about the way you look — although I have to say that every part of your body I can see looks as good as ever." Maura blushed, and Cris paused a moment before continuing.

"Maura, after what we've been through, I don't think I'll ever forget what's really important here. I love the part of you . . . the very essence of your being that makes you who you are. And no matter what kind of body you use to contain that essence, my feelings for you will never change."

Maura smiled and pulled her legs up onto the bed, easing her body down next to Cris's. Once her form was parallel to his, she rested her head on his shoulder and flung a still somewhat weak arm across his chest.

"Oh, Cris, after what we've been through, we can face anything now. No matter what lies before us, we'll tackle it together — as people. We can look to tomorrow instead of worrying about today."

"You bet," said Cris softly. "We have a lot fo look forward to . . . together." A part of him wanted to exude blind optimism, but he knew that's just what it would be: blind. The worst of times was over, he told himself, but there was a lot of work ahead for the survivors of the human race — and even more work for this pair of former Cyborg Commandos and others like them who had to learn how to use their bodies all over again and readjust psychologically to being ordinary human beings.

Then he stopped himself. Hell, he thought, forcing his lips into another thin smile, there's no such thing as an ordinary human being. Every one of us is special, unique . . . and at the same time, we're all part of the same team. We're all in this together. And together, we can do *anything.*

* * *

A long, long time would pass before the Master would acknowledge — admit — what had happened in the battle for planet Earth.

Never before had It been forced to deal with defeat, and the only thing that kept It going were two words it repeated over and over:

Never again. . . .

Authors' note

Players of the CYBORG COMMANDO™ Game will notice some minor differences between specific aspects of the game rules and the way those same aspects are described in this and the other CYBORG COMMANDO books.

These apparent discrepancies are intentional and not meant to cause any confusion or concern among game players. As in other cases where role-playing game environments have been "translated" into novelizations, it was deemed necessary by the authors to deviate somewhat from the strictures of the game for the sake of telling an entertaining story centered around the actions of a few major characters.

The story lines in the books are *based on* the same premise and the same background that serves as the foundation for the game — they are not directly *drawn from* the game rules. If all the readers of the books who are also players of the game can understand and appreciate this distinction, they will be able to enjoy both types of works to the fullest.